1001 GREAT STORIES
VOLUME 2

GW00708162

1001 great stories

volume 2

Edited, with a Note,
by Douglas Messerli

GREEN INTEGER
KØBENHAVN & LOS ANGELES
2006

GREEN INTEGER BOOKS
Edited by Per Bregne
København / Los Angeles

Distributed in the United States by Consortium Book
Sales and Distribution, 1045 Westgate Drive, Suite 90
Saint Paul, Minnesota 55114-1065
Distributed in England and throughout Europe by
Turnaround Publisher Services
Unit 3, Olympia Trading Estate
Coburg Road, Wood Green, London N22 6TZ
44 (0)20 88293009

(323) 857-1115 / http://www.greeninteger.com

First Green Integer Edition 2006
Editorial organization and content ©2006 by Douglas Messerli
Back cover copy ©2006 by Green Integer
For the rights to the individual fictions, refer to the last
page of each story.

All rights reserved

Design: Per Bregne
Typography: Kim Silva
Photographs (clockwise, top to bottom): Mohammed Dib, Niccolò Tucci
(by Virginia Schendler), drawing of Oliviero Girondo, Hagiwara Sakutarō

LIBRARY OF CONGRESS CATALOGING IN PUBLICATION DATA
Douglas Messerli, editor [1947]
1001 Great Stories, Volume 2
ISBN: 1-931243-98-0
p. cm – Green Integer
I. Title II. Series III. Editor

Green Integer books are published for Douglas Messerli
Printed in the United States on acid-free paper.

Contents

Note

The publication of the first volume of *1001 Great Stories* in October 2005 confirmed public interest in a long series of short stories and supported my belief that such a series of books would be popular. This, the second volume, continues what will be the dominate pattern of the series, a wide-ranging selection of international figures covering the centuries. Among the noted figures of this volume are the early and mid-20th century American author, Djuna Barnes; the contemporary and recently deceased Algerian-French novelist and poet, Mohammed Dib; the Greek story-teller, poet and novelist Andreas Embiricos; contemporary Czech dramatist and writer Daniela Fischerová; early 20th century Japanese experimentalist Hagiwara Sakutarō; German modernist novelist and storyteller Georg Heym; Anglo-American novelist Aldous Huxley; Slovenian author Lojze Kovačič; and Italian-American storyteller Niccolò Tucci.

As with the Green Integer PIP (Project for Innovative Poetry) series of anthologies, I envision this short-fiction series as an entertaining and educational project that will help English-language readers discover the joys of international writing and to recognize their own writers within that international context.

Looking into the crystal ball of future issues, I see a large double issue devoted to twenty Norwegian tales (planned for volumes 3-4), and others of German, U.S., Italian, Austrian and Russian fiction, as well as the general selections typified by volume 2.

Once again many individuals must be thanked for making this book come to life. Diana Daves once more proofread the series, while Kim Silva did her magic of typography.

I would particularly like to thank the editors of Catbird Press, Xenos Books, Libris, White Pine Press, and New Directions for their help with permissions. Gilbert Alter-Gilbert, Nikos Stangos, Alan Ross, Neil Bermel, Hiroaki Sato, Susan Bennett, and Miriam Drev must be feted for their excellent translations.

—*Douglas Messerli*

Djuna Barnes (USA)

Djuna Barnes, born in 1892 in Cornwall-on-Hudson, New York, began her career as a journalist and story writer. After living in Paris for several years, she returned to New York, where she became a legendary figure, living the life of a near-hermit, in Greenwich Village

Today Barnes is most recognized internationally for her masterwork Nightwood *and for other works of fiction, including* Ryder *and* Ladies Almanack. *She also wrote plays, most notably* The Antiphon, *published by Green Integer, and shorter dramas collected in 1995 as* At the Roots of the Stars. *More recently, her poems have been collected in* The Book of Repulsive Women *and elsewhere.*

"A Night Among the Horses" first appeared in A Book *in 1923, and again in the collections*

A Night Among the Horses *(1929) and* Spill-way *(1962). It appeared also in* Collected Stories *of 1996, published by Sun & Moon Press.*

Barnes died in New York City in 1982.

A Night Among the Horses

Toward dusk, in the summer of the year, a man in evening dress, carrying a top hat and a cane, crept on hands and knees through the underbrush bordering the pastures of the Buckler estate. His wrists hurt him from holding his weight and he sat down. Sticky ground-vines fanned out all about him; they climbed the trees, the posts of the fence, they were everywhere. He peered through the thickly tangled branches and saw, standing against the darkness, a grove of white birch shimmering like teeth in a skull.

He could hear the gate grating on its hinge as the wind clapped. His heart moved with the movement of the earth. A frog puffed forth its croaking immemoried cry; the man struggled for breath, the air was heavy and hot; he was nested in astonishment.

He wanted to drowse off; instead he placed his hat and cane beside him, straightening his coat tails, lying out on his back, waiting. Something quick was moving the ground. It began to shake with sudden warning and he wondered if it was his heart.

A lamp in the far away window winked as the boughs swung against the wind; the odor of crushed grasses mingling with the faint reassuring smell of dung, fanned up and drawled off to the north; he opened his mouth, drawing in the ends of his moustache.

The tremor lengthened, it ran beneath his body and tumbled away into the earth.

He sat upright. Putting on his hat, he braced his cane against the ground between his out-thrust legs. Now he not only felt the trembling of the earth but caught the muffled horny sound of hooves smacking the turf, as a friend strikes the back of a friend, hard, but without malice. They were on the near side now as they took the curve of the Willow road. He pressed his forehead against the bars of the fence.

The soft menacing sound deepened as heat deepens; the horses, head-on, roared by him, their legs rising and falling like savage needles taking purposeless stitches.

He saw their bellies pitching from side to side, racking the bars of the fence as they swung past. On his side of the barrier he rose up running, following, gasping. His foot caught in the trailing pine and he pitched forward, striking his head on a stump as he went down. Blood trickled from his scalp. Like a red mane it ran into his eyes and he stroked it back with the knuckles of his hand, as he put on his hat. In this position the pounding hoofs shook him like a child on a knee.

Presently he searched for his cane; he found it snared in the fern. A wax Patrick-pipe brushed against his cheek, he ran his tongue over it, snapping it in two. Move as he would, the grass was always under him, crackling with twigs and cones. An acorn fell out of the soft dropping powders of the wood. He took it up, and as he held it between finger and thumb, his mind raced over the scene back there with the mistress of the house, for what else could one call Freda Buckler but "the mistress of the house," that small fiery woman, with a battery for a heart and the body of a toy, who ran everything, who purred, saturated with impudence, with a mechanical buzz that ticked away her humanity.

He blew down his moustache. Freda, with that aggravating floating yellow veil! He told her it was "aggravating," he told her that it was "shameless," and stood for nothing but temptation. He puffed out his cheeks, blowing at her as she passed. She laughed, stroking his arm, throwing her head back, her nostrils scarlet to the pit. They had ended by riding out together, a boot's length apart, she no bigger than a bee on a bonnet. In complete misery he had dug down on his spurs, and she: "Gently, John, gently!" showing the edges of her teeth in the wide distilling mouth. "You can't be ostler *all* your life. Horses!" she snorted. "I like horses, but—" He had lowered his crop. "There are other things. You simply can't go on being a groom forever, not with a waist like that, and you know it. I'll make a gentleman out of you. I'll step you up from being a 'thing.' You will see, you will enjoy it."

He had leaned over and lashed at her boot

with his whip. It caught her at the knee, the foot flew up in its stirrup, as though she were dancing.

And the little beast was delighted! They trotted on a way, and they trotted back. He helped her to dismount, and she sailed off, trailing the yellow veil, crying back:

"You'll *love* it!"

Before they had gone on like this for more than a month (bowling each other over in the spirit, wringing each other this way and that, hunter and hunted) it had become a game without any pleasure; debased lady, debased ostler, on the wings of vertigo.

What was she getting him into? He shouted, bawled, cracked whip—what did she figure she wanted? The kind of woman who can't tell the truth; truth ran out and away from her as though her veins wore pipettes, stuck in by the devil; and drinking, he swelled, and pride had him, it floated him off. He saw her standing behind him in every mirror, she followed him from show-piece to show-piece, she fell in beside him, walked him, hand under elbow.

"You will rise to governor-general—well, to inspector—"

"Inspector!"

"As you like, say master of the regiment—say cavalry officer. Horses, too, leather, whips—"

"O my God."

She almost whinnied as she circled on her heels:

"With a broad, flat, noble chest" she said, "you'll become a pavement of honors...Mass yourself. You will leave affliction—"

"Stop it!" he shouted. "I *like* being common."

"With a quick waist like that, the horns will miss you."

"What horns?"

"The dilemma."

"I *could* stop you, all over, if I wanted to."

She was amused. "Man in a corner?" she said.

She tormented him, she knew it. She tormented him with her objects of "culture." One knee on an ottoman, she would hold up and out, the most delicate miniature, ivories cupped in her palm, tilting them from the sun, saying: "But look, look!"

He put his hands behind his back. She aborted that. She asked him to hold ancient missals, volumes of fairy tales, all with handsome tooling, all bound in corded russet. She spread maps, and with a long hatpin dragging across mountains and ditches, pointed to "just where she had been." Like a dry snail the point wandered the coast, when abruptly, sticking the steel in, she cried *"Borgia!"* and stood there, jangling a circle of ancient keys.

His anxiety increased with curiosity. *If* he married her—after he *had* married her, what then? Where would he be after he had satisfied her crazy whim? What would she make of him in the end; in short, what would she leave of him? Nothing, absolutely nothing, not even his horses. Here'd be a damned fool for you. He wouldn't fit in anywhere after Freda, he'd be neither what he was nor what he had been; he'd be a *thing*, half standing, half crouching, like those figures under the roofs of historic buildings, the halt position of the damned.

He had looked at her often without seeing her; after a while he began to look at her with great attention. Well, well! Really a small mousy woman, with fair pretty hair that fell like an insect's feelers into the nape of her neck, moving when the wind moved. She darted and bobbled about too much, and always with the mindless intensity of a mechanical toy kicking and raking about the floor.

And she was always a step or two ahead of him, or stroking his arm at arm's length, or she came at him in a gust, leaning her sharp little chin on his shoulder, floating away slowly—only to be stumbled over when he turned. On this particular day he had caught her by the wrist, slewing her around. This once, he thought to himself, this once I'll ask her straight out for truth; a direct shot might dislodge her.

"Miss Freda, just a moment. You know I haven't a friend in the world. You know positively that I haven't a person to whom I can go and get an answer to any question of any sort. So then, just what *do* you want me for?"

18

She blushed to the roots of her hair. "Girl-ish! are you going to be girlish?" She looked as if she were going to scream, her whole frame buzzed, but she controlled herself and drawled with lavish calm:

"Don't be nervous. Be patient. You will get used to everything. You'll even like it. There's nothing so enjoyable as climbing."

"And then?"

"Then everything will slide away, stable and all." She caught the wings of her nose in the pinching folds of a lace handkerchief. "Isn't that a destination?"

The worst of all had been the last night, the evening of the masked ball. She had insisted on his presence. "Come" she said, "just as you are, and be our whipper-in." That was the final blow, the unpardonable insult. He had obeyed, except that he did not come "just as he was." He made an elaborate toilet; he dressed for evening, like any ordinary gentleman; he was the only person present therefore who was not "in dress," that is, in the accepted sense.

On arrival he found most of the guests

tipsy. Before long he himself was more than a little drunk and horrified to find that he was dancing a minuet, stately, slow, with a great soft puff-paste of a woman, showered with sequins, grunting in cascades of plaited tulle. Out of this embrace he extricated himself, slipping on the bare spots of the rosin-powdered floor, to find Freda coming at him with a tiny glass of cordial which she poured into his open mouth; at that point he was aware that he had been gasping for air.

He came to a sudden stop. He took in the whole room with his frantic glance. There in the corner sat Freda's mother with her cats. She always sat in corners and she always sat with cats. And there was the rest of the cast—cousins, nephews, uncles, aunts. The next moment, the *galliard*. Freda, arms up, hands, palm out, elbows buckled in at the breast, a praying mantis, was all but tooth to tooth with him. Wait! He stepped free, and with the knob end of his cane, he drew a circle in the rosin clear around her, then backward went through the French windows.

He knew nothing after that until he found

himself in the shrubbery, sighing, his face close to the fence, peering in. He was with his horses again; he was where he belonged again. He could hear them tearing up the sod, galloping about as though in their own ballroom, and oddest of all, at this dark time of the night.

He began drawing himself under the lowest bar, throwing his hat and cane in before him, panting as he crawled. The black stallion was now in the lead. The horses were taking the curve in the Willow road that ran into the farther pasture, and through the dust they looked faint and enormous.

On the top of the hill, four had drawn apart and were standing, testing the weather. He would catch one, mount one, he would escape! He was no longer afraid. He stood up, waving his hat and cane and shouting.

They did not seem to know him and they swerved past him and away. He stared after them, almost crying. He did not think of his dress, the white shirt front, the top hat, the waving stick, his abrupt rising out of the dark, their excitement. Surely they must know him—in a moment.

Wheeling, manes up, nostrils flaring, blasting out steam as they came on, they passed him in a whinnying flood, and he damned them in horror, but what he shouted was "Bitch!," and found himself swallowing fire from his heart, lying on his face, sobbing, "I *can* do it, damn everything, I can get on with it; I can make my mark!"

The upraised hooves of the first horse missed him, the second did not.

Presently the horses drew apart, nibbling and swishing their tails, avoiding a patch of tall grass.

Reprinted from *Collected Stories* (Los Angeles: Sun & Moon Press, 1996). ©1996 by the Estate of Djuna Barnes; Edition and revisions ©1996 by Douglas Messerli. Reprinted by permission of Douglas Messerli and Sun & Moon Press.

1001 Great Stories

Mohammed Dib (Algeria/France)

Born in Tlemcen, Algeria, Mohammed Dib moved to Paris in 1959, upon completion of his great fiction trilogy L'Incendie. *Dib has written numerous novels, short stories, and collections of poetry. Among his major works are* Dieu en barbarie, Que se souvient de la mer *(translated into English as* Who Remembers the Sea*),* La Danse du roi, La Nuit sauvage *(translated as* The Savage Night*),* L'Enfant-jazz, *and, in English and French, the poetic novel* L.A. Trip: A Novel in Verse, *published by Green Integer.*

In 1994 he received the Francophone Grand Prix, the highest literary prize awarded by the Académie Française. Dib died in 2003, evidently of complications from diabetes.

Beneath the Black Veil

She was nude: covered up, that is, by a per-
verse facsimile of a *haik*—one of those veils
which are traditionally white and which
metamorphose into specters women of flesh
who enmesh themselves in them when they
must go outdoors. It is a custom observed by
the least young, certainly; those of the present
generation, not to mention the generation
coming next, already blithely ignore these
shrouds. To the adolescent set, the veil is
nothing more than an object of curiosity or
derision; they can't see wrapping themselves
like sacks of flour. Just the same, being
"nude" is what continues to be said of a
woman, old or not, who doesn't wear one
while out in public.

Haphazardly bundled around her, like
loosely draped towels, were two or three di-
sheveled and out-of-fashion shifts; otherwise,
this woman was nude. Rigged to a scarf
folded in a band around her brow was a
square of shabby black cloth that dangled

over her face. When I noticed this, I winced inside.

There had spread over the world that morning, an April morning, the moist sweetness of an eye glistering with health and refreshment, and the way to summer seemed open; over with were the sore throats, coughs, colds, and other miseries. And I thought to myself: *It's been a long while since a morning seemed similarly promising and you were disposed to greet the world in a chipper mood while heading towards your office, eh, Mr. Hamad Celaadji, attorney, thirty-four years old?*

That pretty much sums up my state of mind at the time, or at least correlates with what it had been up until that point, which is to say that I lugged along with me, oblivious to the hell existence can be, the exultant certainty that the day ahead held a rendezvous with happiness. Surfeited with the exhilaration of that conviction, I strode along the corner of the Garden of Eden as if it had been set aside as my personal preserve.

The day having started in so auspicious a fashion, I couldn't help but try to put my best foot forward and, to this end, ballasted myself with a good dose of optimism. My brain teeming with the business of litigating all the time and with the pressing affairs of my professional itinerary, I walked without paying much attention where I set my feet, or caring, particularly, either. I didn't bother to think about my trajectory since, adopted long ago, it unfailingly brought me, of its own volition, to my office door. Unhindered from reaching that threshold and all that waited there to assail me, I was beset by a sense of...what can I call it? The unaccustomed? Yes, that's it—he unaccustomed. Something wasn't quite right. All my faith in the morning's promise was subverted by the sense of a presence half-perceived around a corner I had just turned and, compelled by forces beyond my control, I halted after a few paces, and retraced my steps. As if I had known already—though I had no way of knowing—I identified the presence in question. I recognized the manner in which she camped in front of the ruins of a police station recently blown up by a bomb. It was a woman—one to whom I had paid no attention, even though she had undoubtedly been standing there all the while, just as I had dreamed her—naked, with her face covered by a black veil.

I contemplated her, entirely submerged under her Medusa-like spell; I was so caught up, so disoriented by a brusque, almost nauseating shock, that I tripped over myself, and nearly fell onto the sidewalk.

What was she thinking to make herself into such a spectacle? People happening by would shoot her a glance in silence, then keep walking. I was hardly in a position to criticize their behavior: I had had the same reaction myself when I happened past. It's perfectly understandable. For my part, I had my cases to think about, and there was always the urgent need to be at court on time. One gets caught up in the daily routine, as they say; the usual grind into which one's life gets sucked, and where a clean conscience makes its bed. So when I saw her, I was knocked off balance. Indignation, horror—I don't which of these sentiments gripped me with greater violence.

Tall but not strong in her tangle of twisted shifts loosely ribboning in long streamers of transparent pearl-blue silk, and with a scarf wrapped around her head, there she was, and so was I.

I had never seen anything like it. She must have been about thirty—my age—or thereabouts. Some irrational impulse drew me towards her, my profession having habituated me to addressing myself unceremoniously to persons of every stripe.

With voice and gesture, I interrogated, "Madame, if you'll pardon my asking, why are you standing here?"

I was going to add: *in that get-up,* but it was repugnant to me to hear myself utter such words.

Advancing towards her, my hand meanwhile received hers, which she extended trustingly.

"Kind sir, I am awaiting my son's return. He is my only child," she said. Her voice, deadened on its way to me by the black veil, was grave, flat.

I exclaimed, "What! With that covering

your eyes and face? A mask! How do you expect to see him? And besides, is it proper or decent to..."

The hand she had placed in mine she withdrew to pass over the veil which hid her features.

"...decent to be dressed like that?"

But, as I was on the point of adding, *"not wearing that appendage, but nude..."* a kind of tortured embarrassment made me go on to say, "...decent that you should stand, that is, in the middle of the street?"

Without the slightest embarrassment, with a spontaneity which, on the contrary, made, me, Hamad Celaadji, feel embarrassed, she explained, "The darkness into which my eyes have been plunged, and where I wander, will make it easier for me to see him when he starts coming towards me. That boy is my light."

I could think of nothing to say in reply. This conversation left me, nevertheless, strangely dissatisfied, and I inquired, "And where is he? From what direction do you suppose he will show up?"

"That...is just what's bothering me: I don't know. I wait. All I can do is wait. He must pass through this way."

"How long have you been waiting," I asked.

The same words were whispered to me this time in an evasive tone: "I don't know." The veil fluttered feebly as it breathed this utterance.

Then I said, "Wouldn't you like me to guide you...to wherever you think might be the best place to find him? We can look for him together. The city isn't so big that we won't stumble across him somewhere." And, under my breath, I added, "With God's help."

Either having considered the merits of this proposition, or because she saw no point in pursuing our interview, she took me up on my offer, though keeping a strict, stony silence.

After awhile, the muffled, sequestered voice revived and sprang to life again: "It's my curse," she said. "I don't know how to explain exactly."

"Be that as it may," I retorted, "Is it really

possible that you plan to continue to go about the streets as you are?" I was thinking of adding this jibe, for emphasis: *naked, and with that sinister rag over your face.*

She replied laconically, "Why not?"

At this point, my interlocutrice began to sing softly, yet loudly enough to attract the attention of whomever might be passing by, "My son, my son, good people, if you see my son, tell him I have been waiting for him all this time. Charitable souls, tell him his mother is looking for him. Son, you must come back; from my lips, you will hear no reproach. Karim is his name..."

I could not refrain from muttering under my breath: *Saint Karim.*

"Good people," she went on, "Let him know...the Lord will bless you."

Had she forgotten my presence? I suspected she had, but how was there any way of knowing, or even of feeling at ease, when all she did was confront you with that veil-stifled, screened-off stare? The mill inside us begins to churn. Listening to this woman droning her plaint, I was surprised to find myself anathematizing life, though I myself had nothing personally to complain about. And the mill goes on churning.

Behind her mask, no less isolated from the world now as when I first came across her, this anonymous woman took refuge in a mutism apparently without a name.

And if she devoted herself to prayer? At my core, I encouraged her; *pray, pray, for that will bring balm to your troubled heart...*

Then the same incantation began again. Underneath the black cloth, she hummed, "My son, my son...good people, if you see my son, tell him I am always here, right here, waiting for him."

While this was going on, someone approached; doubtless a specimen of her "good people," one of those officious persons born to edify others. Slithering down my ear canal, he warned, "She's crazy. Her son was killed during a bomb attack at the spot where she has posted herself. She has lost her mind and you, you're just wasting your time listening to her maunderings. There's nothing you can do for her."

I turned around to take stock of this individual. Suddenly, without so much as a by your leave, he scuttled off.

I said to the woman, "Come on, we'll look for Karim together. What do you think?"

Without a word, she slid her arm under mine, and let me guide her. With the greatest of ease, she had been transformed from the blind person she had wanted to be, into the genuine article.

We walked along at a casual pace, silently and, in truth, aimlessly. The shocked and bewildered glances, the gawkings and gapings we had to endure leave little room for wonder why we believe ourselves to be descendents of apes! Who such people are and what they think, however, is a matter of complete indifference to me.

After a bit, my companion stopped, pulling me up short at the same time. In a chagrined voice, poignant with regret, she protested, "Oh, Dear. We're going the wrong way. This isn't the direction we should be heading."

Blind beneath her black drapery, she had no way of perceiving whether or not we were getting anywhere.

"What's that," I exclaimed. "In what direction should we be headed, then?"

"We will never find him going this way," she said. "We must go back. For the love of God!"

Without adding another syllable, by a pressure on my arm, she made me turn about-face. Soon it was she who was guiding me.

And before I noticed, we had returned to the place where we'd started.

She sensed my surprise and commented, "This is the place. Here is where I have to wait for him to return. He disappeared at the instant he and I reached this spot." She let go of my arm in front of the same calcinated ruins which were all that was left of the bomb-blasted police station.

The poor, dumb beast. She had become a beast holed up in a lair from which she would never emerge, and who would never again do anything except stand exposed all day in the open street.

The unknown woman intoned, detailing

each word, "He who has shown pity, the Lord will show pity, and repay him a hundredfold. He shall dwell among the blessed because, to the Lord, each existence is precious."

In this manner, she signaled my dismissal. After a pause, quickly drawing a breath, she confided, "Now you must leave. I will find my son."

Such force of conviction! I was the beast; an animal who didn't understand anything except except dirt and dung, when all was said and done.

Before moving off I stood a short distance away, and enveloped the woman with a parting look: in the full light of day she seemed submerged in the blackness of a cave, confined to a cave interred inside another cave, in another city, in another country, where nothing reigned or would ever reign except night, for all eternity. But she, cast in this darkness, this eternal night: what had she done? For what was she being punished? The crimes of others?

The noise of the street was incessant, manifesting who knows what sorts of hopes: perhaps those of recapturing fragments of life which, in its course, always runs faster and faster and farther and farther away, not to mention the view blocked off by a square of black mourning crepe. In the distance, a cry arose, dominating this racket: "Fresh mint! Fresh mint!"

The cry grew in volume as it drew nearer. "Fresh mint! Fresh mint!"

Then there supervened a sort of hunchbacked dwarf with a fat bundle of bushy green tufts balancing at the end of a long, rough-hewn pole.

They went up the street, he and his cry, and passed on. As I watched, the dwarf quickly disappeared in the crowd. His musical cry lingered in the distance, with its melancholy refrain: "Fresh mint! Fresh mint!"

Car after car streamed past, and it struck me that they were more plentiful than usual.

I had abandoned the mysterious vigil-keeper, and left her abeyant in her den. Could anything more be done for her? The words of consolation spilling from my mouth assuredly had for their object nothing more than the appeasement of my own conscience. Vain, derisory words, which left a flavorless taste of solitude on my tongue.

*

* *

"Hamad! Hamad! What's with you? Come on, let's go!"

Splintering the dream into which I had strayed, this voice shouted to me from the wings and jerked me offstage. It wanted me, it refused to be ignored, it wanted to make itself understood. And the echo of my name, lancinating, offered itself the rejoinder, "Hamad, Hamad, it's nothing! It's just a dream! Come on, wake up!"

The voice climbed from there up the high walls and, as I listened, said to me, "A new era is beginning. Life will start again truer than it was on the other side. But this life will be more obstinate than a beast, a beast who, rather than jump over an obstacle, knocks down the walls."

And I recognized the voice; it was that of Saliha. Yes, we call ourselves, she and I, by our given names; that isn't done in our families; we do it. Saliha is my wife.

Now present in my dream, she declaimed, as if for the sheer delight of it, while all space seemed to rejoice in sympathy, and resonate around us throughout infinity, "Hamad, it's nothing! You were only having a dream!"

Detached from me, another me never stops listening or keeping an eye out for tricks. But what was it doing, this hand poised on my shoulder which shook me rudely, urging me to "snap out of it"?

My body detonated and thrashed about, I opened my eyes and goggled at those eyes hovering above me. As I broke out of my dream, Saliha broke out of it, too.

In those eyes, where I contemplated myself, was a look that was luminous, smiling, as much upon the visible universe as upon inner enigmas. I didn't recognize my voice when I asked her, "What's the matter?"

"What's the matter," she shrilled. "You suddenly let out a scream to make one's hair

1001 Great Stories

stand on end, and then you started sobbing like a soul in perdition. What were you dreaming about?"

I said vaguely, "It was just a dream. It's over now."

I inhaled slowly, drawing in some deep draughts of air and, as if slapped on the back, sat bolt upright, my lucidity recovered.

I couldn't see Saliha anymore.

Then I saw her come back, with a glass in her hand.

"Take it," she said. "It's fresh water. Drink it, it'll make you feel better."

I drank, attentive to the descent of this freshness in my body, and I made the emotional affirmation, "Saliha's voice, the water—one is no less refreshing than the other." Curious effect of dreams. That arbitrariness which neither foresees nor cares what happens when they swallow us up. One can chase through them forever, but never accomplish anything except to turn oneself inside out. Even when the outcome is firmly in hand, all one has to do is be aware of it to be abruptly awakened.

I finished off the water. Saliha was right: it made me feel better. Meanwhile, as I started to set down the glass, an inept laugh half cut off by hiccoughs took hold of me. That woke me up!

"Had I been dreaming," I asked, mockingly. "And how!"

"To judge from your screams, it must have been a nightmare," said Saliha. "One of those terrible nightmares where you see yourself grabbed by goblins."

"You can say that again," I replied.

"And what was it about, this nightmare," Saliha asked. "Describe it."

"Well, for no particular reason," I began, "I was hastening towards my office when, in the street, I came across a woman, naked, but wearing a square of black fabric concealing her face..."

"That's ghastly," Saliha interjected.

"I was certain," I went on, "that, behind her veil, she was watching me all the while. I felt that her eyes were fastened on me. And then, and then...I don't know...I've forgotten the rest."

As Saliha didn't insist, I stopped my story there. We went back to bed. Little by little, rose the measured respiration of a sleeping female. Light breathing, confidant, trusting, suitable for restoring a man lying alongside of her whom sleep has eluded. Because even if I had let go of my dream, it hadn't let go of me. After the part I had already told her, I felt it was best to spare Saliha the rest of the horrifying tale. As I gazed among the shadows of the room, I saw myself standing again next to the woman with the screen of soot pulled over her face, and began to talk to her, to offer her advice and assurances. She had to go home, I told her sternly, and wait there for her son to return. To expose herself in such a fashion was undignified for a respectable woman. At the very least she should put on some proper clothes and tidy herself up, etc....etc....

"But my child will come back to this spot, not somewhere else, and who will find him, if not his mother," was her simple reply.

My counsel hadn't dampened her determination. A long silence followed. "Such silence," I dreamed. "From it, anything might crop up." And in the same voice as before, a somewhat faded voice, she suddenly inquired, "The mother of a lost son—perhaps you would be interested to know what she looks like? Would you like to see, would you like to know what she looks like?"

She leaned her masked face towards mine and, with the same atonic taciturnity, she drily continued, "Would you?"

The strange person posed this question so dramatically and so skillfully that, recovering my powers of speech all at once, I blurted, "Yes, I would!"

With a flick of her wrist, she lifted the black veil and held it up with her fingers. There was nothing underneath. That is to say: there was a blank, a gaping chasm; it was not the contours of a face, but a dark hole, in its place, which loomed in front of me.

What she'd done, no doubt in a spirit of concession mingled somewhat with an air of defiance, barely lasted a quarter, a tenth of a second, but this sliver of time encrusted itself in pure immutability before the veil was re-lowered again. I cried, "Help! Help!"

I cannot recall who it was who came to my aid. I implored men, women, whomever passed by who might be of assistance in protecting me against this abomination.

Such had been the finale of my dream—monstrous. What good would it do to tell Saliha?

*

* *

I went back to my office that morning. I took the same route: the same one where she had burst into my itinerary. But now, I strode along with the firm intention of verifying if a lady wearing a mask was present there, and if I had accurately recollected the events of the day before and not been the victim of a hallucination; in another words, I was determined to confirm that I hadn't experienced some sort of waking apparition whose sole reality derived from my dream of the previous evening. I hardened myself as best I could and, with a circumspect, if somewhat oppressive curiosity, I set off fatefully towards the point of the putative encounter, telling myself, "It was after all, apparently just a nightmare. It needs to be dragged into the light of day, to be aired out. It's something I have to do."

Coming into view, it seemed as if the rubble of the police station destroyed by the terrorists' bomb were still smoking and as if she, keeping her post on the sidewalk, were a sentry. I looked at her, without moving, from the sidewalk opposite. She broke off the lamentations which I had heard her make the day before; I had the intimate conviction that she recognized me, and that she'd fixed me in her gaze through her veil—like when a crazy person is staring at you and you can feel the stare even when your back is turned, and even though you don't know where the stare is coming from.

Each of us looked up and down the street, scanning one part, then another, but I had left my face exposed and was the only one of the two to do so. What could this mean? Could my face be seen unless it were drawn to an absent face, a face which wasn't there? An absurd question, and even more absurd to formulate it.

Violently, I tore myself away from this sad spectacle and, lowering my head, I went on my way. But a few steps afterwards, I understood that my life was replicating itself from the outside in.

©2005 by Green Integer, translated by Gilbert Alter-Gilbert. Reprinted by permission of Green Integer.

Andreas Embiricos (Greece)

Born in 1901, Andreas Embiricos worked in the offices of the London-based Byron Steamship Company (which belonged to his family) between 1921 and 1925. He later moved to Paris, where he joined the surrealist group of André Breton. *Among his many books are* Blast Furnace *and* Argo, or the Voyage of a Balloon. *"Excelsior or the Rose of Isfahan" appeared in* Grapta *in 1960, and was translated as* Amour Amour *and published in Great Britian in 1966. Green Integer republished this volume in 2003.*

Excelsior
or the Rose of Isfahan

It was spring and I was in a public garden. We all knew that someone would be arriving that day, but no one knew who it was we were expecting, or the exact time of his arrival. We all felt, though, that the arrival was at hand, because the sky was exceptionally clear and all the birds sang madly. The grass was springing up everywhere—almost visibly to the naked eye. Abundant clear water splashed copiously from the fountains. The secretion of saliva in my mouth increased all the time. My heart beat violently in my broad chest.

Most people hung about in the avenues and in the big square of the town. I preferred, however, to wait in the public garden. Without knowing why, I had the feeling that I would be better off there, rather than at any other place, especially as I had chosen a small hill on which to stand, a hill situated on the outskirts of the park from whose slopes I could watch and follow the arrival.

My impatience grew, soon developing into uneasiness. In spite of this, being a passionate lover of tender young girls and charming young women, I found a way to cope with my impatience. I began a detailed study of three girls, all in a similar state to my own, equally impatient and on edge about the arrival. The three girls were extremely beautiful, their ages fluctuating between ten and thirteen. The first held a magnolia in her hand; the second, a May-bug; the third, and most beautiful, wore an azure cape, a large straw hat on her blonde head, and on her lips an enigmatic and, at the same time, enchantingly sweet smile.

A short way off from us, two governesses were sitting on a bench and discussing things together. A blind beggar nearby stretched out his cap and prayed to God that the sins of the dead relatives of passers-by be forgiven.

"I can't make out who's coming today. What do you think?" said the first governess.

"I don't know," answered the other. "He is coming though, he is coming....I am certain of it."

"Yes, he is coming! He is coming with glory and with myrrh," said the beggar, interrupting his begging for a moment.

"But who, after all, is coming? Who?" the two governesses asked the beggar with obvious impatience.

The blind man frowned for a while, then, turning his eyeless face towards the sky, replied:

"He who is expected from the East, from Isfahan."

The two governesses looked at each other amazed.

"What does Isfahan mean?" a very young boy, holding a yellow balloon tied to a string, asked his governess.

The first governess opened her mouth to answer but at that moment trumpets rang out. The governess got to her feet dumbfounded. The crowd, electrified, began to chant:

"He's coming....He's coming...."

After a while, from one end of the public garden to the other, from one end of the town to the other, loud rhythmic cheers began to go up from the assembled people.

"He's co-ming....He's co-ming...."

"He's coming!...He's coming!..." I also shouted, without, however, withdrawing my gaze, even for a moment, from the three girls, especially from the one with the azure cape.

"He's drawing near!...He's approaching!..." Two of the three girls, jumping about on the grass, were shouting enthusiastically with the crowd.

"He's coming!...He's coming!..." cried the entire population.

Only the third girl, her straw hat now on her knees, remained silent, an ardent expression on her face. She was incredibly beautiful.

"He's coming!...He's coming!..." the small boy repeated like a parrot, jumping spastically up and down. Then, turning anxiously but lovingly towards his governess, he cried out loudly:

"Quick...quick...please...I want to pee..."

The governess, however, ignored the child's entreaties. Conscientious though she was, her attention was completely drawn elsewhere. Deaf to the boy's cries, she also was waiting ecstatically for a sight of him who was expected, whose arrival was sounded on the trumpets, adding to the expectation and feeling of celebration an unmistakable undercurrent of universal eroticism.

While the young boy continued his entreaties, cheers were suddenly heard in the distance. Then, and only then, did I succeed in tearing my eyes from the young girls who, at that moment, in order to get a better view, were climbing the bench at the top of the grassy slope on which we were standing. Overtaking them, I took up a position three or four yards in front of the bench, and looked down at the road. The cheers were closer now; they were getting louder and louder. The multitude vibrated. A detachment of policemen was trying to hold back the crowd, which was about to spill from the pavement on to the wide avenue in front of the garden.

At that moment, from an easterly direction, a glistening landau appeared, drawn by two fine horses. The coach was approaching triumphantly. The crowd was boiling over in excitement. The carriage seemed to contain someone very special. But the smart coachman, with his huge body, prevented us from making out who was inside.

The people, unable to contain themselves, were crying out:

"He's arrived! He's arrived!...Hurrah!... He's arrived!..."

In the midst of the pandemonium, the blind beggar's words came to my lips and, along with other cries, from time to time I shouted out:

"He's coming!...He comes with glory and with myrrh...."

The carriage drew even closer, until at last its passenger appeared before my dazzled eyes.

Among cries and shouts of joy, exclamations of rapturous admiration were now heard. In the landau an exquisitely beautiful young girl of 11 or 12 was standing on the back seat, all by herself, completely naked. Smiling, she graciously greeted the multitudes to her right and to her left. Her blonde hair was being ruffled in the breeze, the nipples of her young breasts were erect, while nestling between her white thighs, among her golden pubic hillock, lay, rosy, protuberant and throbbing, her tender vagina.

The people cheered and shouted with joy. I could not believe my eyes. The young girl riding in the landau was none other than the beautiful girl with the azure cape who was with us in the park only a moment ago!

Still remembering the prophetic words of the blind beggar, I cried out, my soul on fire:

"Glory be to you, Rose of Isfahan! O Beautiful One, Full of Grace, Glory to you."

Tears of joy filled nearly everyone's eyes, as well as mine. As soon as the carriage had passed, I turned round and looked at the bench. Only two girls stood on it. The third one, the most beautiful, was missing. Only her azure cape and her large straw hat were in her place. I ran over to snatch the hat and lift it up. Underneath lying on the azure cape was a magnificent rose. I shivered violently as I took it in my hand. A small envelope was pinned to one of its leaves. In the envelope was an extremely delicate prophylactic made of fine elastic and in it a small piece of folded paper. I took out the paper, unfolded it and read it in astonishment. At that moment, I heard someone, behind me, reading out the content of the minute note, which had been written in the handwriting of a child.

"Whoever finds me ought to keep me. I am she whom you have been expecting."

I turned round to see who was standing behind me. It was the blind beggar who had regained his sight and who was reading, over my shoulder, the precious note, the precious message which I held in my hands—I, the luckiest man in the world!

The vast crowd was still delirious.

Nearby the two governesses were kissing each other. The small boy had pissed all by himself for the first time, like a real man, and had joined in the cheering with his shrill, childish voice. A policeman, wild with excitement, was shooting in the air. A middle-aged man was kneeling under an orange tree and muttering passionate prayers accompanied by incomprehensible sighs. Men were throwing their hats in the air. Women and girls were waving their arms, crying or laughing. The blind man's eyes sparkled. I wanted to shout something again but I was so moved that I only managed to cry out, like a whinnying horse. At last, hurriedly clasping the beggar's arm, I rushed madly from the garden, taking the cape, the straw hat, the rose and the precious note with me. Running like mad, I followed the road along which the landau carrying the beautiful young girl had disappeared. A strong smell of roses issued forth from all around and the people frenziedly celebrated in the streets, fraternizing under a magnificent shining rainbow, which had unexpectedly appeared in the clear sky.

Reprinted from *Amour Amour* (Los Angeles: Green Integer, 2003), translated from the Greek by Nikos Stangos and Alan Ross. ©1966 by Alan Ross. Reprinted by permission of Green Integer.

Daniela Fischerová (Czech Republic)

Daniela Fischervá, born in 1948, is a leading Czech writer of the generation born after the Second World War. She is best known for her plays, which have been staged around the world. She is also known for her books for children, screenplays, and radio plays.

Her first play, Dog *and* Wolf, *caused such a political scandal that she was banned from having her plays performed for eight years.*

"The Thirty-Sixth Chicken of Master Wu" was published in her collection of stories, Prst, který se nikdy nedotkne *of 1995, translated into English as* Fingers Pointing Somewhere Else. *Fischerová lives in Prague with her husband and their daughter.*

The Thirty-Sixth Chicken of Master Wu

à V. L.

"Your nephew is here, Master," the serving boy announced in a funereal voice, supposing that it made him sound educated. "He would gladly undergo a hundred more incarnations for the privilege of greeting you."

Wu knitted his eyebrows until their spiky white hairs converged beneath his forehead. He had no taste for yet another commentary on the combination of *sin* and *sa* syllables, but did not see how he could avoid it. The aroma Wu himself had named "porcelain maiden" was surely wafting along the corridors all the way to the court; in all the empire no one else had the skill to prepare the porcelain maiden. Only Wu. Only he! He and only he!

He felt a wearisome pressure in his head, the hollow pressure of several indistinct ideas ("fame—nakedness—nowhere to hide"), but there was no time to consider them: he had just lit the flames, and with painstaking care he was swinging the pan in an arc three thumbs wide and three-quarters-of-a-thumb high. Only thus could the "maiden" truly be released.

"Let him enter."

A tubby, aging youth was standing in the doorway, shifting from foot to foot. He shuffled awkwardly along the wall into the room. His belly was soft and he teetered on long, thin legs like a wading bird.

"It's hot," the youth said reproachfully.

"Lots hot," he added after a moment.

He took off his hat and mopped his balding head and his short, chafed neck with a none-too-clean handkerchief. The odor of his sweat intermingled with the porcelain maiden, and only Wu's six-year monastic education in controlling his inner demons allowed him to hide his distaste. He was nearly certain no one would notice that aberrant moment in the final product, but nonetheless all hope of perfection was irrevocably gone. At the most critical juncture, when the pieces of meat first mystically united with the blue-burning sauce of Jena beans and pepper, an alien stench had permeated them—and that never helped matters. Still, Wu said to himself, those two geese—meaning the empress and her oldest daughter—they won't notice it, but as for me, I would never let it touch my tongue.

"Thank you, exalted one, for-stooping-to-my-humble-insignificance," he mumbled. It took far less time to say than it does to read. Centuries of misuse and age-old affectation had ground this common idiom down to a few muddled, utterly meaningless syllables. The poet looked at the round chair as if wondering what to do with it, and then sat heavily down.

"Whatcha cooking?" he said without interest.

What a question! It stung Wu, but lightly, like a flea. Everyone knew the porcelain maiden. Even his nephew had eaten at least his weight's worth; he should know that aroma by now! What if I asked him: so you write poems, is that it? Never heard of them. No one recites them!—His inner demons toyed briefly with the idea of saying this out loud, but Wu did not have the time just now.

"Dinner for the empress," he answered calmly.

The meal was now almost ready. All that remained was to pour it into stone bowls rubbed generously with a bitter root. Wu did not usually rub the bowls himself, but yesterday he had caught a plump little girl peeling the root with fingernails that were horrendously dirty. He was so infuriated that he whacked her with a large ladle. She whimpered for a while and this morning made herself scarce—well, she was evidently afraid, probably off complaining to some hysterical aunt of hers that she couldn't take that old madman anymore.

Alone! All on my own! the demons wailed, and from the height of a child's arm Wu began precisely and ever so carefully to pour the pungent substance into the steaming bowls. When the moist maiden touched the sizzling stoneware it underwent a final, triumphant tremble. The vitreous meat writhed and congealed, as if it wanted to flocculate, but it held fast, its surface splitting slightly open. It now looked like the frozen skin of a very pale girl, with a polished tinge akin to that of old miniatures.

Wu knew this was the only way to achieve a gradation of flavors. In the meat's tiny cracks, the juices had not uniformly hardened, and the crust had become a concentrate of the concoction's spicy apex: a plume of taste, its coloratura.

Wu, as always at that moment, remembered the day he had discovered the trick with the hot bowl. He was not quite thirty and had run non-stop out toward the Buried Wells, nearly delirious with a high, ringing joy.

"The empressetta eats too much," the poet said indifferently, undoing his belt to let his belly flop out. "The princessina too. They're glutton-guts."

It was the poet's habit to mutilate the most common of words, as if he didn't even know his own language. And to think his teacher had been one of the empire's most famous grammarians! At fifteen Wu's nephew had put out his instructor's eye in a scuffle and was immediately exiled to the provinces.

Only his family connection to Wu and, at the time, Wu's strong hand, had enabled him to return years later.

The poet stuck his hand under the silk.

"Have you spoken with the censor?" he asked, yawning. From the wild rippling of the ribbons he appeared to be scratching his belly most energetically.

Ah, so that's why you're poking around here! Wu thought, irritated. You've come to find out whether this year they'll finally have a public reading of your...your...He hesitated, but the only thing that came to mind were some words mutilated in his nephew's style, so he stopped trying to pin down the concept. Well, you can wait, boy, you can wait. I think I already do more for you than I should by letting you parasitize the family name—and heaven knows it's never done anything for me. But for me to dishonor it further by advancing your your...It was the same problem as before, and Wu abandoned his ruminations.

"The censors," he said severely, "are

drowning in work just now. Over a hundred poems came in for the emperor's birthday celebration contest. The censors have locked themselves in the library and have been studying them for days."

His nephew stared sleepily at the smoke-stained ceiling as if this answer had nothing to do with him. The porcelain maiden became more delicate by the moment; it evaporated into oblivion like a dream before waking, and what was left behind was a taste just as evanescent, haunting and hollow. His nephew could probably no longer smell it, Wu realized, and soon, after twice the time, it would desert Wu as well. How many times have I lost her already, and where does she disappear to? I'll never know.

"The emperor will probably disappear," his nephew said suddenly, in the expressionless tone he always used. "I figured it out by doing a structural analysis of the last hundred years of court poetry."

*

Here there should be a brief aside. It concerns the translator's responsibility for the words *structural analysis,* for the words *censor, parasitize, coloratura* and, in the end, for the majority of others.

There are two basic ways to translate what has not yet come to be and what no longer is. One is with the eternal present's abbreviated arc, in the belief that the sense of words and things endures and, like Zeno's arrow, hangs in flight. The other keeps to Babel's model, clinging anxiously to the literal meaning of individual words confined to the solitary cell of their place and time. We choose the first method, but this does not mean it is the better one. Wu's nephew definitely did not say *structural analysis,* but if we were to take this to extremes, then he was not a *nephew,* but a *second left blood with male sound,* because that is how the language in question characterizes this relationship.

The word *censor,* in its professional sense, is roughly the same as we picture it today. *Head censor*—so we know in advance what is meant—is not a profession, but a title, a pedestal of honor and imperial might, and, it must be said, quite a high pedestal indeed.

*

"What did you say?" Wu sputtered. He was not asking about the emperor's fate; he refused so thoroughly to take this seriously that he forgot it at once. "Where did you happen on the last hundred years of court poems?"

"I have them." The poet shrugged.

"Where did you get them from?" Wu pressed him.

"From the bibliotheca. It's not like anyone reads them; the dust on them was a finger deep. I simply took them."

Wu raised his eyes to the heavens. The poet suddenly became wary. He glanced around and then leaned over.

"I figured it out!" he whispered in a theatrical whisper. "If only it's not too late! Sit down, let me explain."

Wu did not sit down. He was an old man and deeply disliked getting up again afterward. At this hour, when the servants had taken the dishes away and swept out the drifts of ash, the kitchen was quiet for the first time all day. Tense, vigilant, Wu devoted his nights to experimentation. He slept little, and many a time it was only when the stars had left their fatal conjunctions and the great crimson parrots had begun to squawk over the eastern gates, that he finally put aside his bowls and ingredients and plunged his worn, slender tongue into water.

"They've compared him to an elephant eight hundred twenty-two times already!" the poet announced with a passionate fervor Wu had not seen before—at least not since the time when, as a boy, he had shouted at Wu that he'd been in the right in that argument with his teacher and a poke in the eye could-n't alter this basic fact. Except then he'd been fifteen.

"I'm sure as sure can be! I've checked it over countless times! No one must ever do it again, ever! It's...it's death!"

Wu stared in surprise at his nephew's pockmarked skin: agitation had made a child-hood scar reemerge like a long-gone, wind-blasted epitaph on a gravestone.

"Why shouldn't they?" he said evenly. "I'm not an expert on poetry, but as a simile it seems to me both accurate and respectful."

The poet clenched his fists.

"The devil take accuracy! To hell with respectfulness! They've gone too far! And soon there will be retribution!"

Wu had no idea what his nephew meant. His allegations seemed likely, even though it would never have occurred to Wu to count. Comparing the emperor to an elephant was so common that no one gave it a second thought. The elephant's suitability derived from its beauty as well as from its strength, not to mention the esteem it had enjoyed in the empire since time immemorial. The commemorative poems all the empire's poets entered in the emperor's yearly birthday contest positively teemed with elephants, every time. But Wu still could not conceive what anyone could have against this. It had always been thus, ever since he could remember, under the emperor's father, grandfather, and probably even beyond, until the past's thread was broken by war or earthquake.

"Poets don't create anymore!" his nephew hissed. "They just steal from each other! They're worse than grave robbers. They're hyenas!"

"Careful, boy! Take care!" Wu raised his voice. "No celebratory poem was ever stolen! The emperor's censors are ever so strict on that point! The punishment for stealing a contest poem is worse nowadays than for trespassing!"

His nephew, seated, stomped his feet on the floor.

"Last year Mr. Hayo won with the poem: 'The emperor's might is like the elephant leading his herd'! Does he think we've forgotten that twenty-eight years ago Asum's verse ran: 'The emperor's might bursts forth like a raging elephant'?"

"There's no comparison!" Wu adamantly insisted. His profession had given him a fine sense for the subtleties of variation. "An elephant on his own behaves completely differently from one leading a herd. Everyone knows that!"

His nephew's pale eyes grew ever so slightly paler.

"It's a conspiracy!" he whispered. "Betrayal by intellectuals. They want to destroy the emperor!"

There had been times, entire decades, when the force of these words would have swept the kitchen clean, but just now the empire lounged in a sort of political siesta. There had been no war for almost twenty years. This was mostly because the emperor was an old man (Wu, by the way, was exactly one day younger), and the most faithful of his men had kept their posts and grown old along with him. The law of the jungle and hungry battles to the death now raged further down, among the younger clerks, who were still freshly predacious and thankfully far from power. But here, at the top, where a few fading elders quivered like silken flags, the scales of danger and guilt expressed themselves in symbols, not in deeds. Here battles were fought with smiles and insults, transgressions of etiquette and double entendres. A glance averted at the right moment could change the course of history. For years no blood had boiled.

"Uncle! Uncle!"

His nephew hoisted himself up to his full shapelessness, like a prophet.

"Uncle! Do you know how to write the word *thaut?*"

He pulled a piece of paper from a fold in his robe and shoved it under Wu's nose. On it was the character *emperor*. Well, fine, it was also the character for *thaut*.

Wu scrunched his wrinkled eyelids quizzically. He sensed this was a trick question, the sort of riddle the poet had loved as a child, and Wu had no desire to be tricked. In their language, the words *emperor* and *thaut*—the second signified some sort of half-forgotten mythical beast—were not pronounced the same, but for unknown reasons shared the same character. Everyone knew this, and because *thaut* appeared very rarely in ordinary speech, it did not cause the least confusion. No one gave it the slightest thought.

"See? See?" his nephew whispered, and his scar darkened with blood. "It was such a beautiful beast! It had golden horns and could fly through the air! It's an eternal shame. Is this how the elephant will end up?"

Wu shoved the paper away.

"I don't know what you have against elephants. The emperor enjoys being compared to them. Our emperor is quite fond of elephants."

"Well, I'll tell you," his nephew announced. He stood up, crumpled the sheet of paper, and threw it in the fire. "You I can tell, you won't betray me. In the time of one of the emperor's ancestors or, to be more precise, at the end of his grandfather's reign, the most common simile was that the emperor was like a thaut. Handsome as a thaut, wise as a thaut, and miraculous as a thaut. They went on and on, poets and others too. Then the emperor himself took the title Thaut."

"Where did you learn this?" Wu challenged him.

"I told you. At the bibliotheca."

"Who let you borrow poems from the reign of the emperor's ancestors?"

"I borrowed them on my own!" his

nephew said in exasperation, as if unable to concede that there was anything odd about this. In truth, it was as shocking as borrowing the princess to study at home.

"No, I will not protect you! Never! I won't lift a finger for you!" Wu shouted.

His nephew bent over toward him secretively.

"I've discovered something no one else knows. Even my teacher didn't tell me about it. Once, you see, the word *thaut* was written differently. It had its own separate character!"

"Don't count on me once you're in hot water! I'll disown you! I should have done it long ago!"

"It was only when the emperor started calling himself Thaut that the two words came to be written with the same character. And at the same time this metaphor vanished from poetry, at once, instantly, as if the earth had swallowed it up! Don't you see? How could anyone still write: the emperor is like a thaut? Such a sentence would be pointless! Not only would it have been incomprehensible—it would have looked awfully clumsy as well!"

In spite of himself, Wu remembered that his nursemaid had once told him about the thaut. She swore she had seen it with her own eyes. If he remembered correctly, it was something like a chamois, but more clever, and able to fly. An elephant is much stronger.

"Then they began to compare the emperor to many other things. To the buffalo, to the sun, even—once!—to wheat. It was a great time for poetry!"

Oh no, Wu sighed inwardly. *Sin* and *sa* syllables. If I don't throw him out, he'll start reciting his latest brainchildren.

"But for fifty years now they've been babbling: the emperor's an elephant! The emperor's an elephant! They haven't learned from what happened before. You can't repeat anything too often, or it destroys itself. Back then it just happened, do you hear me! just happened to destroy the thaut. But this time it will destroy the emperor!"

Two things struck Wu during this tirade.

First: what an unendearing person his nephew was! Second: the monastery superior would have made short work of him. The boy would have stopped his trickery, one two three!

"We think..." Excited, his nephew leaned right over to him and swallowed his final consonants, like a country boy. It was a bad habit picked up in the provinces. "We believe that the thaut never existed. That it's just a beast from old fables. But how do we know that, eh? What if it did exist, back then, what if it soared through the mountains and had golden horns? Who in God's name can say? What if it only disappeared when the emperor appropriated its name, whipped it out from under the thaut's nose, as if he had the right to it, as if it belonged to him? What if it had to disappear just because they were already so similar, there wasn't room in the world for both of them, and the thaut simply lost out?"

Wu's nephew thumped his fist against his knee.

"But the elephant is strong. He won't give way. Not the elephant!"

Wu still could not understand him. His nephew didn't even completely understand himself, because he was trying, tediously and without the necessary intellectual apparatus, to define a concept that had not yet come into existence. It was—let's call it—the concept of redundancy, and with it the allied concepts of innovation, informational esthetics, and possibly the exhaustibility of repertoire. Not only did these concepts not yet exist—there was not even a hint of the force which, in time, would coil in a loop around one of these matters and by sheer pressure compel the word into being.

Neither Wu nor his nephew could know that this would only come to pass in their part of the world a good two or three hundred years hence. But by then this palace would be overgrown with grass from end to end, and the great-grandson of the eastern gate's parrot would have died of homesickness in a foreign land no one in the palace had ever heard of. Both knew only this: that Wu's nephew was bitterly humiliated by his insignificance, and that he would never achieve fame—and he himself understood his own words less and less the more these feelings clogged them up.

"There are lots of elephants," the poet grinned cunningly. "They look quite plucky, don't you think, uncle? The last few weeks I've been going to watch them, observing them for hours."

Then he leaned over so far that his nose touched the clasps on Wu's chest, and Wu quickly took a step back. For years he had found physical intimacy unpleasant.

"Say 'the emperor's an elephant'!" his nephew pleaded passionately, but then, without waiting for an answer, he granted his own request: "The emperor's an elephant. The emperor's an elephant. The emperor's an elephant."

He waited a moment, as if listening for some subtle echo, and then shook his head:

"Nothing. It has no meaning anymore. There is no helping the emperor."

What he said was very simple. All the words he used were familiar to Wu. They weren't even mangled. But Wu did not understand them. Not only that—in the true sense of the word Wu had not even *heard* them. He had never thought of them and never considered anything even close to them. Later, in the time of the parrot's great-grandson, everyone would recognize them, and in three further generations they would be mute with age. But now they were mute with newness and Wu felt only their strangeness, a feeling so common for an old man that it told him nothing at all.

"Run along," he said. "Go home. I want to be alone now."

His nephew shuffled to his feet without protest. Suddenly he looked as expressionless as always, excepting the brief fever of his last speech. He gazed at length around the room, as if he had forgotten where the door was, and then said in a slight whine:

"Uncle! When will you be speaking with the Head Censor?"

Oh heavens, not again! Requests, petitions, mumbling, sniveling, muting of conversations as I come through the door, vanishing around corners, muttering behind my back, tugging at my sleeves—

"The Head Censor does not visit me!" he answered sharply.

"But couldn't you...for old times' sake ..."

Suddenly Wu's blood boiled in his veins.

"Out!" he roared. "Scram!"

His nephew left; Wu did not see him out. He merely watched the young man's hunched back totter down the hall, and shook his head: how old he looks! At thirty-one I looked my thirty-one years, but I aged differently. There was a powerful current of youth, and a powerful current of old age surging against it, and their waters mixed with a roar, like a dam bursting. But him—he's a ditch full of dried-up mud.

He saw this image with absolute clarity, but he did not think it, and if he had had to describe his nephew's aging, he would not have found the word *water,* nor the word *ditch,* nor the word *current.*

*

When Wu entered the years of River (also known by the flowery name "midday mountain time," signifying a man's most powerful age, from forty to fifty), he created and discovered things with great ease. He was singularly ambitious and, thanks to his years in the monastery, remarkably disciplined. His inventiveness seemed bottomless.

The annual tradition of preparing a completely new chicken dish in honor of the emperor's birthday began at this time and for many years seemed completely unproblematic. He felt sure that he would have new ideas as long as he lived, and that it would always be in his power to create something that did not yet exist. Wu never presented his guests with the pinnacle of his art at any particular time. In the fermenting abundance of his inspiration, he offered one of many possible versions. He saw a geyser of creation inside himself, an inexhaustible source of innovation.

At first he had no inkling that *Wu's new chicken* would become a custom the whole empire would make its business. He did not even know that this era—this court, this land, this configuration of planets—worshiped tradition and misused it as a defense against its own unpredictability. Time hurtles forward, changes howl furiously at the boundaries of existence, tatters of the ages whirl in the winter wind, but one thing remains certain: year in, year out, on the emperor's birthday, dignitaries from all seven provinces gather to taste the new chicken of Master Wu.

Chicken was as integral to the emperor's birthday as the emperor himself. A ritual had developed around the tasting. Understandably, it was a great honor. The number of guests varied over the years, but had finally stabilized at twenty-two of the most powerful, who on that day were permitted only tepid water for breakfast, whom the heavens forbade to take lunch, and who, with the rising of the tiny autumn evening star, would finally receive a deep bowl containing five or six morsels of the new chicken.—Wu sometimes wondered whether he had succeeded in educating even one true gourmet who would esteem his art as only an expert could. Certainly he had terrorized those twenty-two people to such an extent that they slavered at the sight of the meal and did not speak until they had swallowed it.

For years Wu had no idea that, in addition to fame, this custom would earn him the title of chamberlain (to use Zenoic language), then later high chamberlain, and finally a nebulous position as one of the most powerful men in the empire, whose choleric shrieks over his skillets decided the fate of the court more surely than did any government petition.

Even Wu himself could not pinpoint when he had first lost his certainty that this year's recipe was completely different from the last. Perhaps it was the chicken with sesame, nine years ago. The sesame was in and of itself nothing novel. Its originality resided elsewhere: from the moment it hatched, the fledgling was fed a special mixture of herbs and grains soaked in hot infusions. It was incredibly ingenious and horrendously laborious, but even so, the result did not have a particularly innovative taste. The twenty-two guests consumed their portions with no less enthusiasm than before, which relieved Wu somewhat, while arousing in him an ill-focused feeling of contempt.

After all, there had been years that were incomparably better, more inventive, more distinctive. For instance, the clerical election year, when he had found a truly exceptional flavoring, known ever since as *I mourn you, lost love, my betrothed Li.*

(A note: these names were not Wu's doing; it was the emperor's literary office that thought them up, or more accurately classified them according to a classical key. The betrothed Li came from a fable, probably connected in some complicated way with the ruler's ancestry and thus especially in favor. But Wu himself did not know the story; it did not interest him and he had certainly never mourned her.)

Li owed her fame primarily to the fact that she was made from chickens not raised in their land. Wu had imported them from the south. Their long necks gave them a foreign air, true, but above all it was the masterly work Wu had done on them.

En route, several of Wu's chickens had expired from the tremendous heat. When he discovered this, a fearful rage overcame him, and he nearly beat to death the two laggards sauntering alongside the wagon. He was around fifty at the time, quick-tempered and quite brutal. However, after incalculable effort, hours suffering over the slow flame of enlightenment, he realized how to make use of the chickens' slightly spoiled tinge, and created a dramatically unusual dish.

It was then he learned the secret that as a deviation from the norm, a mistake serves just as well as anything. For a time he even flung himself into new experiments involving deliberately spoiled ingredients, and it must be said that, despite the morbid domain, he made some interesting discoveries.

Equally splendid was the year of the princess's engagement, when he had mixed the meat with the sweetly pungent juices of a local tree and made what was almost a dessert; and then the year (he could not remember which) when he froze the chicken until the pieces tinkled delicately in the bowls; and the year of chicken mousse whipped into a stormcloud. There were years when all he had to do was concentrate and an idea came as quickly as a cringing servant handing him a fork.

But for four years now his inspiration had lain mute. Five, actually, since the celebration was just around the corner. In five years he had not managed to find a new flavor.

There were moments when Wu thought he could not bear his impotence anymore. He did not give in to despair, because he was foremost a man of battle, but for the first time he was faced with the very worst: battle with the nonexistent. If he had seen a way forward, he would have followed it till he dropped but for five years now it seemed he would drop right where he stood.

Many a time he had been willing to believe that the circle had closed, that there were no new flavors to find. Incidentally there was a sect of astrologers, right in the palace, trumpeting the coming end of the world, "once all the words have been said," but the attitude toward them was one of silent reserve.

Wu still lived in the hope that once more the circle would break, that he would resist the grip of the nonexistent and find an herb that no mortal had ever tasted. He would get hold of something banal, something right in everyone's view, but hidden by the magic of its obviousness. Then the source would be forced to yield and to gush forth from the center of its being. But the celebration was approaching, and as the sun rose he would stand over a pile of dirty bowls and then fall reluctantly into the fitful sleep of the elderly, of which he rarely remembered a thing.

There was a certain comfort in the fact that he did not really have to expend the effort. He knew full well that not one of the guests had a gustatory memory that could span thirty-six years.

Over time Wu had realized that it was he who was abnormal. But he had not yet fathomed that aside from his exceptional culinary imagination, he was a rather ordinary person. His tongue was a miraculous floating island in a sea of superficial education, unrefined sensibility, and quite unexceptional intelligence. He was like those feeble-minded twins from Kosice who can multiply five-digit numbers in their heads but will never understand how a toilet flushes. Or—going further back in history!—like the Paris garage attendant who speaks thirty languages fluently but only reads comics and invoices, because his spirit reaches no farther than the metal grating of his garage.—Wu knew that he could offer any of the last thirty-five chickens without anybody recognizing them, but that option still seemed impermissible.

All it took to make him soak his deathbed in sweat was to remember how last year he had stood all day in the Meadow Pavilion, staring for hours into the water. The low, heavy sky turned gray toward night, and the raging river carried with it wrecks, carcasses, beaten trees, and drooping clusters of water narcissus.

Here is how this ignoble story unfolded. He had announced chicken stuffed with stalks of river greens, but the day before the celebration the river flooded and the plans had to be abandoned. Everyone understood, and no one even raised an eyebrow. Wu alone knew why specifically river greens, which, incidentally, were sour and unpalatable. Eight days before—eight days in which he had depopulated the hen-house, like Herod, slaughtering a generation of chickens—a certain foreigner had come uninvited to the court. More precisely, it was a suspicious-looking friend of his nephew's, most likely in flight from some arm of the law, who in the dead of night had begged Wu for shelter. He said that floods had begun on the Five Rivers and that whole villages had fled wailing into the mountains. Early the next morning he disappeared without a good-bye and no one ever saw him again.

Wu had lived long enough to know how to seize the day. With considered trepidation, he announced his river-greens plan the morning after the boy took off. Then there was no alternative but to wait. He did not know who would come out on top, he or time.

He stood for hours, eyes fixed on the horizon. For the first time in his life he burned the porridge. He did not speak for four days.

At least the heavens granted him this one belated favor. The flood came a day early. The celebration ground to a halt, the whole court was thrown into terror, an evacuation was planned. On a day of impatient surrogate celebration, Wu left the palace early and spent the whole day by himself in the Meadow Pavilion, until the empress herself sent a message, telling him to forget about the stupid chicken and to come make her a handful of beer-roasted almonds.

One such memory is more than enough, and the year was again mercilessly drawing toward autumn. The festivities began tomorrow. There was nowhere to call for help. Wu's "where"—more than just a place inside him—had vanished with the same inaudible treachery as his inventiveness.

When Wu was very young, he had been a large hungry container the whole world poured itself into. Later (around fifty, when he was proudest, fiercest, and also unexpectedly powerful, which took some getting used to) he had formed the impression that he and the world were equal partners. It was a matter of his will what and whom he opened up to, and he would take the first move, extending his hand, accepting things rationally and voluntarily. But now the end had come. There was nothing to contain. He had had what there was to have. He was living off himself alone. The world's nozzle had gradually shut off. These days no one gave him anything at all.

His outside world had narrowed to the smallest possible dimensions, the mere shell of a corporeal body which moved with him through space. But recently even this had been further constrained. He never left the kitchen, banquet hall, and the two adjoining corridors. In the day as he slept, at night as he paced from corner to corner like a wild beast, he was plagued by the imminence of his fate. Day after day, time lost its patience. The world was as cramped as a small shoe. In addition, Wu was extremely nearsighted, although no one even suspected it, and thus he had learned to live in the immediate, ever more strictly attuned only to what was within his reach.

They had already painted the great staircase vermilion in honor of the emperor's birthday. Wu locked the kitchen and transferred the burden of daily work onto his staff. Once or twice he sent out for spices. He had them bring large quantities of ice. He requested a bucket of river sand and a tiny vessel of white ointment used only for cosmetic purposes.

In the final three days nobody saw him. A cloud of black smoke would occasionally pour from his windows, and then a cloud of white smoke. Bowls were frequently heard smashing against the wall.

*

Night had begun. Wu was tossing out a greasy ladle. The basket by the door—as always at this time—overflowed with similar utensils. Suddenly there was a quiet knock.

With a glass stick slightly flattened at one end, Wu scooped up some red porridge. Then he closed his eyes. He had heard the knocking, but still did not react. It had been many years since anyone visited him at night, and there was no reason suddenly to start believing in ghosts.

Carefully, he wiped the porridge onto the middle and, a second later, onto the tip of his tongue. For a moment he stood with his tongue stuck straight out at attention and imbibed the waves of his breath, then began sibilantly to roll them back up. Just as the taste poured over his upper palate like a carpet of sparkling colors, someone banged on the door again.

Freeze, Wu thought. Freeze like a lizard on a greensward. There's no one I want to see. No one has the right to take away my final night.

Quietly he rinsed out his mouth and, with a hunter's concentration, set off on the trail of the taste still quivering on his palate. He had often done this. Mornings would find him walking from wall to wall, mouth agape like a gargoyle, flicking his tongue to dispel the last impression, which often slipped to the very edge of pain.

He knew himself exceptionally well. The monastery had given him a thorough and—except for a couple of insignificant trifles—an anatomically correct understanding of his body, but he knew the worn honeycomb of his tongue best of all. He and his tongue, in fact, had embarked on a strange dual relationship, as when the ego distances itself from one of its parts to be able to experience it better—even at the price of having that part abuse its deceptive autonomy and take on its own life. It was a relationship that could take over one's soul or nature, a relationship full of emotions, naive guardianship, anger, and lack of understanding.

There might have been happier moments in Wu's life, but none were more fulfilling than these minutes spent between shimmering shadows, when he stood in taut concentration, scraping his tongue against his eager gums, trying with all his might to understand. To feel, distinguish, know, assimilate. And again he would set out on his usual route from wall to stove, his fiery tongue flicking out of his mouth like some frenzied divinity.

"Wu?" said a hesitant voice from the darkness. And then I again: "Wu?"

Wu froze. Something in his saurian stillness moved slightly. In the whole court, in the whole palace and the whole wide empire, there was no one aside from the shades of the dead who was allowed to call him by name alone. As he raised the latch, he sucked back his sharp saliva with a hiss.

"I knew," said his guest, making a gesture of greeting with one narrow palm, "that I would find you here at this time, Wu."

Wu stood silently, his hands in his sleeves, watching the empire's Head Censor fold up the material of his robe with precise, academically spare movements and then sit down facing him. For a few minutes both old men remained silent.

Outside an angry beak squawked. In the darkness there were many sounds Wu did not recognize. The sentence the censor had just spoken was the first one between them in thirty-three years.

"Wu," the censor eventually said—impersonally, as if relaying an unclear message—"tomorrow your nephew will be executed."

*

The role of this imperial censor in the history of the empire's poetry—and, in a way, of the whole world's poetry—was far from insignificant. In his fertile years he ruled his language's marketplace. History traditionally pigeonholes him as "a cofounder of subjective poetry," but that "co-" is deceptive, for the others who co-founded it missed our censor by hundreds of miles and dozens of years.

Now the censor slowly slipped his hand underneath his robe. He drew out a sheet of paper.

"He entered this in the emperor's birthday contest."

His face was in its way perfect—so perfect that it is hard to report what sort of face it was. It was so cultivated as to be a sort of abstraction: not degenerate or decadent, but an ineffable harmony of features, a small hollow of silence at the very summit of its consummation.

Wu took the sheet from the censor. It was scribbled from margin to margin in a familiar hand—careless but without lightness, illegible without grace. He raised the paper to his eyes and felt ashamed, with the preposterous vanity of old men who have not grown old together. He saw instantly that it was some sort of trick. The first stanza ran as follows:

> *The Emperor*
> *is an emperor*
> *is an emperor*
> *is an emperor.*

The second:

> *The Emperor*
> *is like an emperor*
> *who is like an emperor*
> *who is like an emperor*
> *that is emperor.*

The third stanza is more or less untranslatable, for the construction governing the words *emperor* and *emperor* can be translated either as *nothing but* or *precisely such* or also *most highly similar* and a few other variants. In older translations we sometimes find the possibility...*he and only he!* and in the contemporary form of the language (in what is left of these etymological seeds) this construction confirms the complete identity of two mathematical elements.

The fourth stanza is the most chaotic and can only be understood in a logical and linguistic trance. It says, roughly:

> *If the Emperor,*
> *who is emperor*
> *and likewise is like an emperor*
> *and is nothing but an emperor*
> *(he and only he!)*
> *were not emperor*
> *who is like an emperor*
> *and nothing else*
> *than emperor himself,*
> *there would be no emperor.*

"What is it supposed to mean?" Wu said without even raising his eyes. "Has he gone mad?"

"Oh no...I do not think it is exactly that," the censor replied in that featureless tone that never conveyed more than he wished.

"Then why bring it to me?" Wu burst out in annoyance, fixing his eyes on the censor. Even the censor did not know about Wu's poor vision; he did not realize that the gaze fixed so directly on him saw only an indistinct outline, and that it was this which gave Wu such a firm sense of security. Wu was aware of the secret power of the nearsighted: this was how he stared at the servants when the bowls weren't hot enough, and at the princess when she tasted her food.

The other old man responded with a shapely curve of his fingers, which in the language of gestures meant *I defer to you,* as if indicating that he could certainly answer, but was giving Wu a chance to come to it himself. Wu knew this maneuver all too well from years past. Two ancient tricks dissolved mutely into one another, and for a while there was quiet. When they finally spoke, their words came together.

"The emperor is most ungracious just now," the censor said.

And Wu: "Does my nephew know?"

The censor shook his head. Then he added unexpectedly:

"That's why I'm here. Explain it to me."

"Me? What's there for me to explain?" Wu tossed the paper onto the floor. His eyebrows bristled like blades of grass. Without even knowing why he was so furious, he felt his old anger welling up inside.

"Why me?"

"I hoped," the censor said soothingly, "I hoped you'd know something about it. That's the only reason I dared disturb you."

"I don't know anything!" Wu snapped. Acrid smoke rose, burning, through a crack in his memory. "It's mishmash, no head or tail. It's nonsense!"

"I do not recommend executions," the censor replied, his laconic gesture of release indicating utter resignation, "and it is not in my power to overturn the sentence. But I would like to understand for myself something so...so..."

He hesitated and then added tentatively:

"Something so...exceptional?"

As to the censor's role in the history of poetry, he is among those who are, as they say, a step ahead of their time. The censor achieved this in a very strange way. He stepped ahead of his time without that time even noticing it was being stepped over. The censor's genius lay in the inconspicuousness of his actions. His adroit strategy tamed the world's vicissitudes and inconspicuously overturned the course of an era.

The poetry of the temporally bounded enclave that spanned the old men's birth consisted of purely objective military epics. A more diligent analysis than ours would reveal its song-like format, its stereotypical plot schemes and, most of all, its marked poverty. The same heroic fragments predominate time after time, and the poems are as alike as two peas in a pod. For generations no individual spirit had come forth.

It would not be precisely true to say that the censor played the same role in his time as Sappho did in Greece, for he formed a channel from one style into another and was king in both. He established himself in official poetry, even as a young man imposing on it a certain pervasive lightness without distinguishing himself from it in any special way. Only when he had made his name, when he had become a significant participant in the imperial Word, did an unheard-of note begin to creep into his work: private life and emotion.

At first it mimicked existing traditions so precisely that no one even noticed it. Its quantity increased only gradually, with a diplomacy usually reserved for altering word order in government documents—but suddenly, without that generation's ever expecting it, they found the censor's tone had become the voice of the century.

Today, when, through none of our own doing, we understand better, we know that the censor was truly a great poet, and prefigured an age in poetry probably fifty times longer than the age he himself attained—which was quite advanced. His poems, especially those of his *midday mountain,* are widely read and critiqued to this day. Even now the best of them can, in their depth and fervency, stand up to the highest achievements of all future times, and placed next to them even a nineteenth-century *poète maudit* seems a bit too heavily starched.

But the most wonderful part was that the censor's contemporaries did not know about it; the censor did not disturb or insult them, as such harbingers tend to do. The change from the monotonous racket of military campaigns to hysterical confessional trembling is so leisurely that the enlightened modern reader studying the censor's work cannot avoid the impression of a clear plan and exceptionally adroit staging. A historian of our time, a young Swede, aptly called it "ecstasy by flowchart."

"Wu, speak, please—if you can, of course," the censor gently pleaded.

At fifty the poet in him had fallen silent; he obtained a government post and the track of his poetry suddenly disappears with no explanation.

The birdcalls grew louder; outside it was deepest night. Midnight flared down from the heavens in a twinkling of lights. Laboriously and against his own will, Wu dug from his memory snippets of their absurd conversation.

"Did the boy visit you today?" the censor asked, but it did not sound very much like a question.

"Why do you ask if you already know?"

"I haven't had you watched, I'm thinking it through. Wu, there's not much time before dawn. The execution will be secret, so as not to disturb the celebration. Did the boy tell you anything about his poem?"

In a tremor of anger Wu felt himself nodding to the censor. He tried to prevent it; he did not want to comply, and he hated the feeling that the censor was concealing something from him. Arrogance, peremptory pride— once again he knows best! It was always thus, always—and thirty-three years hadn't changed anything at all.

"He's gotten it into his head that the emperor will disappear," Wu snorted. The censor's placid face immediately tensed.

"Disappear? Why?"

For a moment he resembled an old bird, a slender, withered raptor.

"Because there are too many elephants in our poetry," Wu answered. His masticatory muscles tensed in anger at having to repeat such drivel.

"Go on! What else did he say? Go on!"

The censor leaned over in his chair, and suddenly his elaborate elderly deferentiality gave way to the aggressiveness of a secret imperial lord. His handsome face regained its shape.

Wu had always been far removed from the world of poetry. Although he had been forced to live his whole life at its legally sanctioned heart, it had never held great interest for him. It is fair to say he took note of it only once the censor had initiated the ingenious inch-by-inch shift from propaganda songs to the torment of self-reflection. And strange as it sounds, Wu belonged to that scant handful who noticed the difference. What's more, the change astounded him far more than it astounds us today, from the heights of our foreshortened omniscience of all those years to come.

"The thaut. He went on about the thaut."

"And then?"

"As if I know! That the thaut used to have its own character."

The tall functionary suddenly stood up. With surprising agility he strode over to the stove and grabbed the ash-rake from the wall. While Wu spoke, while he dredged fragments and snatches from his memory, in rapt attention the censor sketched word after word on the dirty tiles.

"Quiet!" he abruptly silenced the chef. "Not another word. Let me think."

He tapped the rake and then squatted. Pained, Wu stared at the narrow back, at the censor in all his imperial majesty, robed in gold from head to toe, crouched in a position Wu associated only with servants, or with little girls, who could toy with things this way for days on end.

Suddenly the censor laughed. It was a laugh full of wonder and distress. Then he shook his head and put back the rake.

"Wu," he said politely, "excuse me, I'll be leaving now. But I'd like to know: where does your nephew sleep?

*

When Wu was a bit over forty (he was slightly the elder of the two old men) the censor's existence struck him like a lightning bolt to the head. It happened in late spring, one luminous evening. It is relevant that Wu already thought he was past his peak.

It is true that, from a certain perspective, the censor temporarily became his "number one," despite the fact that Wu never felt toward him any love or affection in the true sense of the words, or even closeness or trust. But still, thanks to the censor (or rather: in the grip of his emotional force field) Wu experienced these feelings more deeply and passionately than ever before.

Long ago, when the censor's thunderous confessional whisper first resounded in the world's Word, Wu knew as little as could be known about poetry. He had never had the slightest need for the medium of words, and treated poetry with the indifferent attitude typical of masters in other professions. He had a simplistic, if by and large correct view of poetry as a secondary accompaniment to music and, of course, as the history of the empire. Wu always vastly preferred wandering tellers of fables and outlaw stories, which no longer fell into that category.

When quite by accident he later heard one of the censor's more intimate poems (he remembers it to this day: it was a clear evening, the sun was pale, the censor was smoking, and the smoke from his mouth rose into the olive branches), he was shaken to the depths of his soul.

The poem that struck him so was not intellectually complex and today would be dismissed as banal. It unobtrusively expressed surprise at a common fact: namely, that there was single encounter, never repeated, which the poet could not forget, while in his heart's memory people he saw every day were far less meaningful. It was essentially just the flip side of the German wordplay *einmal ist kein-*

mal, aber zweimal ist leen dreimal—"once is never, but twice is thrice." Emotional life is exactly the opposite, as we know. There *einmal* is a relatively high card and singularity is the gate to eternity.

(Incidentally, a further note: a few years later, when Wu no longer knew him, the censor finally arrived at the celebration of the sovereign *never,* at the troubadors' *amor d'onques,* which sings the praises of unrequited love. *That which has not happened* always has a slightly unfair advantage over reality. It is hard to say whether the censor knew this from his own experience. It could have merely been logical speculation, in which his beloved leitmotif reached its most extreme point.)

But the poem Wu heard that day was not this far along. Formally it was modest. It revealed the fatal *einmal* in a traditional form full of flowers, meteorological phenomena, and melancholy evening sounds.

Wu was astounded. He was promiscuous by nature, as is common among such sensual beings, and he was also impatient. He had never understood why (in the language of his scullions) he so quickly lost interest in every woman and why repetition deprived physical love of all savor. It was that fateful *einmal* that made the strongest impression; after it, everything else seemed shallow. He was astounded that someone else could feel the same way. He had never spoken of his *einmal*—a thin, middle-aged woman, long ago, when he had trekked across the desert in his youth—to anyone, even to himself. And suddenly someone had said out loud what had happened to Wu, and had said it precisely, rhythmically, openly.

Wu did not understand how anyone could name that mute gust of wind, and not only name it, but broadcast it. It was not chastity or introversion that bewildered him; he was simply and methodically amazed at the shattering of a concept—here, presumably, the concept of poetry. Someone had jumped the hedge of his heart, penetrated his gravitational field. The cook was overcome by shock.

But once that first astonishment had

passed, it was replaced by a much more subtle amazement. Wu discovered that he could identify, more or less, with the majority of the censor's poems, which he only now began to notice. It seemed to him that the censor, by some sleight of hand, could look right into his blindly tumbling soul and then willfully toy with it out loud.

Inexperienced as he was, Wu took every word as an authentic expression of the censor's feelings and was startled by their great similarity. Yet it is worth noting the single, characteristically intractable mistake the impatient cook was making. It is, by the way, an exceedingly common mistake, and even today various psychologies have foundered on it.

Wu had had a rare experience: an alien inner space had been opened to him, one which he had till then been unaware of, but he was only tentatively getting his bearings in it. He accepted it quite simply—we could even say *flatly,* at the expense of its multilayeredness. Wu had erroneously let himself believe that every hidden feeling he found in this other ego had to be made of the same substance. He did not know that hiddenness does not by any means entail depth, that secrets can be utterly superficial. Lacking experience in the affairs of the soul, Wu was fascinated to hear the censor speak of things that were not commonly discussed—which was, incidentally, the censor's primary contribution to literary history. The more the censor's work enthralled him, the more he came to believe that the two of them were a single being. The other man was by some magic speaking for him and, like the wind, stealing the words from his mouth.

Wu put himself into close contact with the censor. With persistence he became the censor's constant companion, in order to get to the heart of the matter. Wu saw the censor as some sort of freak of nature. He studied him like a spice box.

The censor (we will let him keep this title for clarity's sake, but back then he was not yet censor; he obtained that post only once his productive days were past) was a tall, polished, somewhat coolly attractive man. A ring of reserve surrounded him; inside it he had no real friends. He was not married and did not conduct "affairs." The censor accepted Wu's aggressive affections with kindness and a monotonous politeness, and in time he even found a certain pleasure in his debates with the master chef.

This not too close friendship lasted about three years. After all that time Wu was not a step nearer his goal. His tenacity came to nothing. Who is this man? How does he know what I know and yet don't know? And why him?

The more Wu saw the censor, the more the man disturbed him. He simply could not reconcile that restrained—one could even say British—exterior with the fevered cry of his poetry. They spent hours together on the covered terraces, idly gossiping just so as not to lapse into silence. In his work Wu was accustomed to step-by-step analysis; at one point he secretly focused on one after another of the censor's characteristics—his face, tastes, way of speaking—and delved into them with a persistence he had never before applied to another person. But the censor's eyes were expressionless, his hands calm as they poured the wine, and his tastes temperately indifferent.

By the third year he felt the censor was deliberately deceiving him. The further this current of introspection carried him, the more he came to believe that while he conducted his detailed study of the censor, the censor was doing the same to him. In each new poem he found a piece of himself and countless times erroneously ascribed to himself the poem's feelings and states. He experienced an entire range of emotions never before imagined, and he was quick to appropriate each of them, like a hypochondriac does with the symptoms of diseases. In the final analysis, poets everywhere can thank this egocentricity and its uncontrollable tendency toward error for the fact that we tolerate poetry's existence at all.

"How did you think up that poem?" he would turn on the censor during their early evening meetings. "Who were you thinking about? What kind of mood were you in when you wrote it?"

Wu posed the censor questions that are heard all the time on television. He rousted them forcefully from time's womb. The answers that most of today's artists prefabricate as an integral part of their work were at the time beyond anyone's concern. The creator as subject was beside the point. Wu's insistence came across as slightly vulgar.

"This?" the censor would answer with a smirk. "I don't even know. I can't remember."

"When did you write it?" Wu would not be put off.

"Yesterday."

"All at once?"

"No. Before supper and after."

"And what did you have for supper?" Wu would persist, growing louder and louder, until the servants on the terraces stopped to look.

"Duck."

"With what?"

"Something green. Broad beans, perhaps? No, probably string beans."

"What did you think about during supper?"

"I don't know."

"Why not?"

At some point Wu's desire to understand the censor turned into an obsession. He tracked him like a hunter. Day after day he prized intimate details out of him, longed to lay bare his heart, and still failed to get even the most everyday confidences so easily shared among his cooks.

"You have to know what you were thinking! It was yesterday evening! Any idiot knows what happened yesterday!" Wu would shout.

"Aha, now I know. I was thinking about the fact that the west wing is the oldest part of the entire palace. They should really get the roof repaired. The administrator isn't forward-looking enough to anticipate the autumn rains," was his exhaustive, obliging, and empty answer.

As the sunlight over the terrace gradually faded, Wu would wander deeper into ever more inconclusive interrogation. Finally he would stalk off, full of anger, each time bewildered that a poem created not an hour after this tiresome chatter could be a crowning achievement of refined insight and an astounding inner likeness.

At that age Wu was already quite powerful and dangerously irascible. He ruled the fate of hundreds and took hard the feeling that the censor was making fun of him. One day, using a minor palace conflict as a pretext, Wu shouted at him that he'd had enough of his supercilious glances. The censor gave him a kindly smile. In the grip of an insane rage, Wu grabbed a bowl of boiling water and hurled it at the censor's feet. The puddle soaked their boots, which were made of the same thin material. It got him no further with the censor.

*

One day, a month or so after that evening of rage and shards, a short episode occurred which again changed the course of Wu's life.

He was swimming in the pond. It was morning, a bright, early autumn; the water was warm and full of tiny greenery. Wu swam quickly toward the sun, taking pleasure in his small, stocky body. He was so used to thinking of the censor at such moments that his mind had created a sort of feedback loop, checking every impression with the censor's imagined stream of thoughts.

Even now, as he swam, he posed himself the thousandth version of one and the same question: how would the censor feel about this? How would he—who is not me, and yet in some startling way is—perceive this motion, this meeting of water and skin, the glow of September sun on scalp; how would he see the mountain on the horizon, the white cloud? (The censor never went to the pond; he probably did not even know how to swim, but Wu experimented assiduously with every situation, hoping that one day, in one of them, he would find an answer.)

He glanced at the tips of his clasped hands, which surged rapidly forward. And suddenly, as he caught sight of his fingers, unusually pale beneath the water, slightly changed by the refracted light, seaweed wrapped around his ring-finger—suddenly he was outside himself, and outside everything he had ever known. His body dragged him toward the bottom like a weight. He looked up at a mountain towering over him, so alien that it was almost not a mountain. He breathed in as if someone were forcing air into his mouth.

That was all. It lasted only a moment and there is nothing more to say. But during those several seconds Wu realized once and for all that the censor was the censor and Wu was Wu—he and only he!—and that all his efforts were in vain, for nothing he could learn from the censor would ever be anything other than Wu.

We cannot rule out a purely physical origin for this feeling: for instance, a change in equilibrium, which can certainly occur while swimming. Wu tried many times that morning to recapture it, swimming back and forth across the pond, observing himself with great care, but the feeling never returned.

From that day forth he never called on the censor again. The interest that had exhausted him for three years had suddenly subsided. The circle was full and the time bounded by his forty-second and forty-fifth years came to a close.

The palace, of course, noticed this change and ascribed it to a meaningless intrigue unfolding at the time. The censor himself silently accepted the turn of events and probably thought the same, but Wu's life was so marked by that moment of estrangement that he was unable to imagine what the censor might have thought of it, and instead put him out of his head as best he could.

*

Three hours after the censor left, Wu was still in the kitchen, working. He was searching. There was no sense now trying to sleep. It was still as dark as in the very depths of night, but Wu knew that at this time of year dawn came more quickly than an axe blow.

He worked as if entranced. Time dwindled like the smoldering logs. The night was drawing to a close. The confronation he had been waiting for these thirty-three years and which had slipped by only minutes ago had deprived time of all elasticity. Haste possessed him.

Angry and headstrong, alone, without his servants' help, he lifted giant bowls and stoked the stove. It was nearly the death of him. The meat tongs fell on his hand and made his knuckles bleed, but he did not even notice. He pushed time aside.

Wu worked differently than ever before. He stopped relying on external aids. On sauces, spices, fruits, and additives, on all those glittering cosmetics of flavor. He turned to the very fundaments of his art. He focused his attention on the operations he performed every day, on each process, however simple. He investigated the element of fire, the element of water in braising. The hiss from under the pan, the steam on the ceiling, the hot gust from the oven doors. For ten minutes he stood motionless and, eyes closed, fingered the bottom of one of the pots. He penetrated the most primitive components of creation.

It was the most potent hour of the night, the last before dawn. Wu worked like a man possessed. He was certain he would find something. He no longer tasted. Taste was secondary. The meat's very consistency came alive in his hands. It hardened, softened, took on an unnatural brittleness; its very structure gave way, collapsing into other forms of being, and the chicken was already as little chicken as smoke in the sky is a tree in flames. Just before the potent hour gave way to morning, Wu knew that he had found it.

He was putting away his forks in the gray of morning when someone began to knock gently on the door. For a moment his heart stopped. In a lightning vision he admitted the censor, conducted a long and fateful conversation with him—and then opened the door to see his nephew standing there on the other.

The poet was shaking. He was wet and bloated. Before Wu—could recover, the young man had slipped inside like a mouse,

"What do you think you're doing? Out!" Wu roared.

Wu clenched his fists tight. Pain reminded him of his raw knuckles, but he no longer remembered why they hurt.

"Uncle! Uncle!" the boy squealed. Stiffly he pressed his knees together. "They want to kill me! I'm going to be executed!"

The boy's lower lip trembled. Just don't start to whimper, Wu thought. He was dead tired. The idea of tears on his nephew's fleshy and always slightly lubricious lips repelled him. Now, after hours straining his imagination to study the substance's essences and flavors, he would not be able to stand it. He closed his eyes and held his breath.

"What do you want?" Wu asked.

"Executed!" his nephew yelped. "They're digging a pit beyond the ramparts! It's raining! They'll bury me in mud!"

"I repeat: what do you want?"

Wu stamped his foot. The young man instantly sobered up. He blinked, shook his shoulders, and said quite forthrightly:

"Clothes."

"What kind?"

"Doesn't matter. A servant girl's, maybe."

"Who sent you here?"

Wu's nephew sniffled loudly. "The censor. He said you'd know."

In the grayness Wu nodded slightly. The ties binding me to others in this world are fewer day by day, he realized. Other people's paths still cross behind my back, but each day even those are further away.

"There are clothes in the alcove," the young man added pragmatically. "And a cap. And some kind of...basket or something."

Wu sighed. It was part of his old age, of that empty, ever narrowing path, that he could not even remember anything about his servant girl. He groped blindly around the alcove, feeling various sorts of things whose existence he would rather leave be. The minute he ceased to need her each evening, she simply melted into nothingness—and any clothes she did not need were already in such an abyss of oblivion that he probably would not have noticed them if they were right under his nose. Finally he felt a soft material.

"Did the Head Censor have a message for me?"

"No."

When Wu returned to the kitchen, his nephew was lounging on the chair, looking as if he did not know he was to be executed that morning.

"That crook!" the poet announced, his voice full of rancor. "That stuffed old mummy!"

Wu closed his eyes again. He did not want to watch his nephew disrobe. He was utterly exhausted and experiencing a strange feeling: he wanted to go to sleep.

"He's an ignoramus, " the youth continued. "An imbecile. He acted so clever!"

The poet drew in his greasy lips and mewed in an old man's voice:

"'Too soon, young man, too soon. This age isn't ripe for you'—he's a moron!"

Wu did not even realize he had fallen asleep. For an illusory moment he was ten again and a small, frightened monk...creeping through the leaves and grubbing in the wet soil with his fingers—

"I can't stand him!" his nephew mumbled through the clothing's material. "His stench is everywhere. He's crawling with maggots, but won't let anyone else near the trough. It's not like anyone reads his doggerel. If I ever come back, it'll be to spit on his grave!"

The youth said this with the gloomy resolution of the swarthy southern prophets of old. The end of the world is nigh, they most often claimed. But also: the sun will grow cold, the universe will fall into small black holes—and this strange, age-old fascination with the end had always found them hordes of worshipers.

Wu's nephew pulled on a shapeless gray cap.

"Well, Uncle, I'm off."

And then suddenly he burst into caustic laughter:

"And he's still frightened of me! He's scared witless. I know he is! And the best thing is, he doesn't even know why!"

Wu woke up. The young man stood in the doorway in the servant girl's clothes, looking particularly unappealing. The insipid shapelessness of his sex, his age, his character, and the fate that had marked him forever was only heightened by those bedraggled rags, hurriedly fastened and lopsided.

"He told me to go around the pond. Promised to call off the guards."

Wu rubbed his warm, dry eyes. His

nephew casually opened his arms to embrace him. The old man shrank back.

"Run along," he said, exhausted.

His nephew had already stepped across the threshold. But the youth turned around.

"I am the only one, remember," he whispered deliriously, "who could have saved the emperor...and everything. Just me, who is myself and no one else. I and only I!"

"It's dawn," Wu answered.

The morning fog seeped through the partly closed door. Wu moved closer to the oven. He did not even watch the boy totter off and disappear into the gray rain. He forgot him so completely that the young man vanished from his life long before reaching the pond.

Wu carefully brushed off the hot ash. He removed the lid. The substance steaming in the pot did not in the least resemble meat. It was pulpy, shiny white, broken here and there by a vivid pink streak. If his nephew had returned at that moment, Wu would have thought it was the servant girl come to wash the dishes.

*

The palace shone. Lights burned in both its halls. The main impression the majority of guests took away that night was luminosity. Several small children, who were allowed to roam the hall during the festivities, would remember, even sixty years and two sadistic wars later, the gold-tinged glow, the thousands of candles, and the iridescent smoke up near the ceiling.

By the time the emperor arrived, the festivities were almost over. The emperor was an old man, and celebrations exhausted him. He was only a winged golden wisp waving half-asleep over a cosseted empire, dreaming the occasional short, pale dream.

All the winning poems had been recited. Now a small ephebe—the son of a court lady, probably the emperor's bastard child—took the stand and began to read, or rather to chant, the one that had received first prize. He had a strange voice, as tiny as if it were made of foam, and the voice and poem matched exquisitely.

Wu walked among the tables and checked the settings. The twenty-two bowls were already sitting on polished trays; there was a white cloth over each bowl and a waiter was placing sprigs of jasmine on them.

Wu stopped. The poem was rippling down the usual stairway of *sin - sa* syllables like a multicolored runner. Dominating it, as expected, was yet another elephant. This time it was an almost supernatural one, with diamond eyes, golden hair, and a set of classical enchantments skillfully woven into its elephantine anatomy.

This poem is simply beautiful, Wu thought, without the slightest sense of enchantment. "Perfect!" the old empress announced loudly, and in doing so completely expressed his feelings.

When the poem came to an end, there was an appreciative murmur. Everyone bent as if beneath a strong wind, and in their tiny bows to the emperor, empress, and Mr. Hayo, the winner, they made their satisfaction plain.

Finally came the time for the meal. By now the twenty-two bowls were on the tables.

Wu could not help noticing as here and there someone tried inconspicuously to sniff or to ascertain with a brief touch at least whether it was to be a hot or cold dish. An unexpected disquiet seized him. Far away, in the gallery, a spoon fell, and the chilling reverberation of its tone raced sharply down his spine.

It was strange. He had lived a tumultuous life. He had destroyed many people and saved others. Nothing had passed him by. He had known hatred, passion, revenge, power and glory. There were many bodies he had known from inside and at least *einmal* he had experienced a moment of love. Wu had walked through that boisterous throng of people, been covered in their stigmas. But now, at the end, the only people he noticed were those twenty-two utterly alien beings, of whom— other than the emperor, the empress and the Head Censor—he barely knew a one. In most cases, their death would not have given him a moment's pause, and yet now he breathed their breath and suffered their impatience. In a moment, the last great work of his life would vanish into their hidden senses.

Finally the drum rolled. The headwaiters threw back the cloths. The hall fell quiet like footsteps on moss as the guests placed the first morsel into their ceremonially cleansed mouths. The quiet lasted a moment before the whispers began. It was not common practice to speak during this meal, but now a whirlwind of amazement swept round the hall.

Wu saw the guests raise their heads. His ready pride swelled up inside him. He knew full well why the amazement: the substance they had put in their mouths was so utterly unlike meat that tiny scandals were being played out in the delicate interplay of their senses. They had experienced all the world's tastes, but inevitably conveyed by the soft tissue of meat. What crunched between their teeth was fresh pulp.

"Master!" the old empress shouted energetically. She tapped her spoon against her necklace. "Where is that man?"

Wu smiled. He did not try to restrain the waves of proud delight washing over him. The lights blinded him as he strode into the hall, and it was only by memory that he found his way to the fat dowager.

"Listen here, boy," she said reproachfully, "what is this supposed to be?"

"I don't know what you mean," Wu modestly replied. Delays on both sides would only heighten the impression.

"This thing! This is what I mean!" she snapped, poking her finger into her supper. "It's trickery! Sleight of hand! Is this supposed to be chicken?"

From anyone else—even the emperor—it would have been unconscionable, but this powerful, gold-adorned idol had a right to her quirks.

"It most certainly is chicken, O mighty empress." Wu spoke firmly, as if on stage. He noticed fleetingly that the emperor had closed his eyes and was fumbling around the dish with his spoon turned round side up.

"It has been prepared using special, completely new methods in order to celebrate the greatest of all emperors!"

"M-hm," said the empress, loudly enough so that half the court could hear it. Then she leaned over and pulled a ring off her finger.

"Your hand!" she ordered, tapping imperiously on the table. She placed the ring on Wu's bony middle finger. It was far too large for Wu to wear, but he quickly bent his finger like a claw and with a bow retreated from the table.

Everyone stared decorously at this act of heavenly favor, and as if the empress's naughtiness had been a signal to relax, everyone suddenly began to speak and bow in Wu's direction.

"A miracle! In our age of reason—a miracle!" shouted Mr. Hayo, apparently believing that with fame he could relax his standards a bit.

"The crow got the golden feather!" another poet said. "The tear has turned into a pearl!"

In front of everyone Wu finally uncovered his bowl and placed a morsel on his tongue. His pride glowed like never before. It was not the youthful pride of an initiate (no crown of promise weighed him down anymore); it was the sonorous pride of departure. Extinction's mighty vibrations pervaded the entire hall.

Wu knew that, for a few moments, he had called into existence something no one would ever make again, which even now was disappearing from the face of the earth. In a timeless flash he had wrenched his portion from unreality, defied the inertia of all things—and unreality would swallow it along with him.

"You'd never believe it was meat!" someone remarked in an absurdly deep voice, but it was clear that he was being respectful.

Wu devoted himself to tasting this first morsel. As if meditating, he concentrated all his senses on it. He marshaled his attention—the way his superior had taught him, poking Wu in the back with his short cane—guiding it in from the outside, through the gates of sense, where it anchored firmly in his mouth, and then he began to relentlessly pulverize the stimulus.

The impression the meat gave was very strange. You would never believe you were eating meat. You would swear you had a freshly cut stalk on your tongue. Neither would you find it particularly tasty. Just surprising. Its taste was weak, hidden by that moist vegetable frangibility. Its tones were strange. Wu expertly rolled the morsel around in his mouth—and suddenly froze.

"Master Wu is the empire's blessing!" chanted a functionary from the south, once a cruel and merciless man.

The flavor was not new. Wu tensed all over. He knew this flavor from somewhere.

"Wizard!" a voice called from the depths of the hall.

Where do I know it from? Wu asked himself. He felt a tiny cramp at the thought that he had been wrong, that he had plagiarized himself and inadvertently evoked the same flavor twice.

The noise in the hall grew. As if the crowd could not bear the burden of its astonishment, the room echoed with shouts.

It isn't possible! I used a completely new approach. And still the flavor is not new. I did not create it. It came from somewhere else.

"Genius!" the functionary shouted.

"Artist!" added Mr. Hayo.

A youthful, pliable flavor. Joyful and, in its own way, simple. Fresh like moist earth under leaves in early spring. It leapt from the dish like a sound.

Wu, the morsel still between his teeth, put all his powers on alert. Imperiously mustering every part of himself, he wracked his memory—of that moment in his mouth, at the confluence of body and soul—to yield up its secret.

"Well, you've outdone yourself, Master," the old empress said, finishing her portion first, as always. "Out-mastered the master. You've given us something unique to taste. The emperor knows."

What is it? Wu agonized. That fragile consistency. The way it bursts between my teeth, that moist crunching. Juiciness that doesn't splash like when someone upsets a glass, but squirts out of hidden vessels. And in the distance: the cold sound of hunger. A young, rapacious hunger.

The empress clapped. Everyone stood. Wu gave a start. He opened his eyes and suddenly, in a fraction of a second, a white flash of enlightenment swept over him. Hunger! He was hungry! For weeks he hadn't eaten; he had only tasted. At last he knew where he had experienced that flavor.

"Music!" someone called. Small drums sounded from the hallways. Conversations rose like water in a pool. Wu indistinctly saw movements, someone waved to him, someone bowed to him. It was precisely how wild radish tastes. He heard the word *ovation.*

Radish. Suddenly he felt it on his tongue again, the taste of long-ago fast-days.

The servants changed the candles, and for a while the hall floated in a blinding glow. Wu was no longer in doubt. Yes, he had conjured up the taste of radish. During fasts they had secretly gone to pick them. There had been a whole field of them behind the monastery. Oh, the effort! At dawn they had chewed the radishes with children's teeth. Sneaking along the narrow field path...dozens of identically shaven little monks, indistinguishable in the morning fog. The oh so ordinary wild radish. Grubbing in the wet soil with their fingers. Oh, the effort!

Wu remembered his half-year of despair, but also the wonder of the last night, not dissimilar to the firm happiness of youth. Just then, as if the floor had begun to slide out from under him with a clang, his seventy-eight years began to disappear beneath him. All the exertion ever channeled through him from the heavens down to the earth culminated in an agonizing effort to stand up.

A dignitary from the east, whom he barely knew, quickly jumped up from his table.

"O chosen one!" he said, offering an old-fashioned bow, almost to his knees. "O Master, I search in vain for the words...I hesitate to...I couldn't dare to...only my position might give me the right to ask..."

Wu did not answer. He nodded absent-mindedly, to show he was listening, but he heard nothing and groped his way to a row of pillars. His head was spinning. The drummer banged loudly on his drum. The dancing began. Radish.

Time disappearing into time, so many years of self-denial. Those years of effort, plunging into time like a knife into wet clay, had finally yielded up a flavor as simple and old as the world. This madness for the new,

136

this obsession with uniqueness, which had cast him onto this steep path, defying everything that did not yet exist...Wu staggered along the hallway.

"Lead the emperor away!" said the censor back in the hall, in a quiet but very sharp voice.

*

When Wu had fumbled his way down to the foot of the stairs, he heard a shout from the palace. Dimly he saw the shimmering lights cast someone's distorted shadow across the staircase. He did not care what was happening, but before he could pass through the gate, someone gently blocked his path.

"Wu," an all too familiar voice whispered carefully, "follow me. Quietly. Don't turn around."

Wu followed. It was night again, the first night in many years that he had nothing he needed to do. His mind a blank, he paced after the tall figure, strangely slender in the dark, until they reached the garden by the pond. Finally the shadow stopped amid the shadows.

"Wu," it said again, "I don't have much time. Has your nephew gone?"

Wu nodded. He stared at the black ball of branches swaying in the night breeze. Leaves rustled.

"Good. Wu, I managed to alter the charge. He's only been convicted of illegal possession, for removing materials from the emperor's library."

The night, alive with its own life, spoke in screeches.

"It's better this way. That poem...I destroyed it. No one besides the two of us knows about it. You won't say anything about it, of course. It's a solution."

A veiled question was hidden in the censor's words, but Wu merely stared into the gray moonlight.

"Your nephew is lucky," the censor continued. "The emperor is on his deathbed. I think he will not live till morning. Tomorrow there will be confusion everywhere, and before anyone remembers, the boy will be beyond the Five Rivers."

Wu suddenly felt cold. Repetition, it occurred to him, but without the word. He hid his hands in his long sleeves. Multiplication, proliferation. Nothing can wrench from existence that which it does not contain. Although only autumn, it was nearly freezing.

"It's truly better this way," the shadow repeated with a hint of pleading in its voice, which only someone who had studied it diligently would recognize. "I know what I'm doing. Trust me."

"Yes," Wu said absently. Searching. The source, the spring of desire. And all rivers flow to the sea.

"Wu, I have to go back. Will you forgive me?" the censor asked humbly. He retreated a step. Wu nodded. The other old man suddenly placed his hand on his heart and bowed to him in a mute farewell. Wu did the same. For a moment they stood like that in the darkness, bowing to each other, and then the censor turned and quickly vanished among the cherry trees.

Wu sat down on the grass. It was already

moist with morning dew. His nephew, meanwhile, was wandering along the shore of an unknown river, slipping along its muddy embankment, and because he was a person whose destiny was impatience and yearning, he sobbed loudly, breaking his nails on the icy stones. Wu sat, eyes closed, and with strict attentiveness followed the slow disappearance of time beneath his feet until morning, when the long palace trumpets informed the realm of the emperor's death.

"The Thirty-Sixth Chicken of Master Wu," was reprinted from *Fingers Pointing Somewhere Else* (New Haven, Connecticut: Catbird Press, 2000), translated from the Czech by Niel Bermel. ©2000 by Niel Bermel. Reprinted by permission of Catbird Press.

Oliverio Girondo (Argentina)

Born of a wealthy family in Buenos Aires in 1891, Oliverio Girondo spent his early years in Argentina and Europe, traveling to the Universal Exhibition in Paris in 1900, when he was only nine, and where he later claimed to have seen Oscar Wilde stalking the streets with sunflower in hand. For the next several years, Girondo explored various countries, even traveling to find the source of the Nile.

Meanwhile, back at home he had begun writing avant-garde plays, which caused a stir in the theater world of Argentina. In 1922 he published, in France, his first volume of verse, 20 Poems to Be Read in a Streetcar, which shows the influence of the Apollinaire and the Parisian scene. Only in 1925, with the second printing of this book, did Girondo receive attention in Argentina. By this time, the Ultraists, lead by Jorge

Luis Borges, had become a major force on the scene, and Girondo continued his own humorous exploration of that aesthetic in works such as Decals, Scarecrow, *and* Intermoonlude. *In 1946 he married the poet Nora Lange, and began, in his work, to move away from Ultraist ideas, playing with elaborate metaphoric language. As Borges moved forward his more fantasist works and a new generation of poets arose, Girondo was increasingly described as a humorous or even frivolous poet. But in 1956,* Moremorrow *stood as a darker summation of his career, a work that bears comparison with the great Chilean writer Vicente Huidobro's* Altazor. *In 1964 Girondo was hit by a car, and for several years suffered terrible pain before dying of his injuries in 1967.*

Interlunio *or* Lunarlude *appeared in 1937, and was the basis for the film* The Dark Side of the Heart, *directed by Eliseo Subiela in 1994.*

Lunarlude

to Norah Lange

I saw him leaning against a wall, his eyes almost phosphorescent and, at his feet, a shadow much twitchier and raggedier than that of a tree.

How can I account for his weariness, that look of a dilapidated and anonymous house that is known only by objects condemned to the worst humiliations?

Would it suffice to say that his muscles sought relief from the strain of supporting a skeleton so gangly that it was capable of wearing out even the most recently donned clothes? Would it take any special persuading to see that this same artificiality of effect ended up by giving the impression of a mannequin lumbered in the corner of a storeroom?

Eyelashes brimming with the sickly climate of his pupils, he hung around this café where we used to meet, and, rooted at the far end of the table, stared at me as though through a cloud of gnats.

One certainly would not have needed a well-developed archaeological instinct to confirm that I am not exaggerating or overstating the case when I describe the fascinating seduction of his allure as an impudence and impunity recalling something extinct...except that the wrinkles and the shiny veneer of these corroded vestiges, corresponding to the same premature decrepitude suffered by public edifices, were all too real.

Although accustomed to abiding hour after hour in silence, he could at times be prevailed upon to relate some episode from his life, or to recite a poem by Corbière or Mallarmé. Never was it more dreadful to be in his vicinity! Amid the incessant fumes of a cigarette, his voice, full of soot, resonated as if it were belched from a chimney, while his immobility lent him the murky intrepidity of a portrait of someone whom no one remembers any more and his dentures stubbornly persisted in contriving the most grossly inopportune smiles. In vain would we try to bring the content of some verse to life. After the silence of each strophe came his breath of an unmade bed, the misgiving each time his skeleton emitted some noise, while his beard grew with the same susurration as that with which the beards of the dead grow...And for one already on that slippery slope, it took but a gesture or glance, in which we could see something akin to those pairs of stockings that hang in hotel wardrobes next to desperately twisting dickeys, to prompt thoughts of suicide.

Even if we resisted these excesses, on the other hand, how could we contemplate the bramble patch of his wrinkles without imagining all the lost nights, all the hollow and helpless murmurs that, stratifying themselves with the slowness of stalactites, had formed creases of fatigue that not even death itself would iron flat?

In order to survey them from one extreme to the other without losing myself in the process, I found myself forced to examine them with the same concentration with which I follow routes on a map and, thoroughly absorbed by this outward record of his mishaps, rarely heard what he was saying. Even on those occasions when we found ourselves alone, when I didn't miss entire phrases, they reached me with the same intermittence as when, through an opened window, one hears the chopped-up noises of the street. It was useless to refocus my attention! Always some word leaked away, some particular so essential that, before I could answer, I had to undertake an endeavor equivalent to translating an encrypted document. Garnished with the same premeditation as those dishes that arrive elaborately mummified at a dinner table, his dialectic—aside from other things—didn't excessively stimulate my appetite, since he compounded an abusive employment of paradox with an insistence on quoting from as many books as had fostered his fearsome ability to handle rhymes, an ability that he demonstrated often enough by means of a sample of verses as worn out as the envelopes on which he had scribbled them.

Although my lack of appetite reduced my intake to bits and pieces, I was not slow to ingest a number of more or less shady anecdotes from his life: the bankruptcy, followed by the suicide and other accessories, of his father; his transit through two or three jobs; his need to pawn his cufflinks, tuxedo and overcoat; the first symptoms of hunger—little shivers in the back, little mute and desperate cramps; a thousand incidents in all latitudes, in all climes, until he came to Buenos Aires, which, according to him, was a place of marvels! The only city in the world where one can live without working and without money, because there it was the rarest of things to have a bloodletting with no profit, even in the case of the most well-bled billfolds.

Afflicted as it is by chronic anemia, mine could not rectify the matter even though it had taken preventative measures to keep its discharges from being overly copious and frequent. Due to this infirmity I had to maintain this regimen religiously, so that I was stricken by the contrast between his habitual skepticism and his hyperbolic enthusiasm for the country. This is illustrated by a consideration of how, prior to embarking for Argentina, he had imagined it an enormous cow with a million udders swollen with milk, and how, after ambling through Buenos Aires for a few days, he understood that, in spite of its appearance of a bombed-out fortress, it was the offspring of the pampas, with which the river had mingled in order to give it birth.

"Europe is like me," he was apt to say, "something rotten and exquisite; a Camembert with locomotive ataxia. It's useless to try to smear it with bad odors. The land has nothing left to give. It's overly old. It's full of corpses. And, what's worse, important corpses. In vain we try to avoid them. We trip over them everywhere. There isn't a threshold or latch that hasn't been corroded. We live beneath the same roofs where they have lived and died. And as much as it repulses us, we are left with no other remedy but to repeat their gestures, their words, their attitudes. Only a man capable of wearing a crow's wing attached to his forehead, like Barrès, could take pleasure in learning to fornicate in such cemeteries.

"Here, on the other hand, the earth is pure and unfurrowed. Not a churchyard, not a

1001 Great Stories

cross. Here we can gallop through life without encountering more deaths than our own. And if we stumble by chance upon a cadaver, it is so humble that it bothers no one. It lives an anonymous death: a death of the same shape and size as the pampas.

"In the city, life is no less liberated. From all parts blows an air of improvisation that permits us to act on whatever inclination. All anyone talks about is foul depravity. Expectancy takes root in such unfilled fields! Having said that, as one who has blossomed here, I have often felt tempted to do something myself, and you may as well know it! I may even come to be convinced that sweat is as respectable a secretion as is generally claimed. I prefer it, in any case, to the glister of European cities, so polished, so perfect, that no one would consent to move a stone out of place. Their cornices inspire in us an aptitude for excellent manners. Sooner or later they end up lacing us into a straitjacket. It's impossible to commit an error of syntax, to yawn in public, to grab a flowerpot and smash it to bits on the sidewalk."

These sallies, and others of similar stripe, acquired an accent less rhetorical when they referred to some episode of his life. Because of this circumstance or, perhaps, because of the lamentable state into which he had fallen, I hope I will be able to recapture, with adequate accuracy, what he told me the last time we met.

As I recall, it was in one of those cafés that never shuts its eyes. The chairs had already been stacked on the tables so as to relieve their legs of numbness when the waiter, with a gesture that has long since forgotten the countryside, scattered sawdust over the damp tiles.

Seated before a little cup containing a concoction with a certain resemblance to eyewash, a man appeared in doubt whether to ingest it or use it to cleanse his pupils. From head to toe, his person gave off an aura of ruin and calamity so authentic and so thorough that I recognized him immediately. His pallor of ground glass, his beard spun by a spider, his greasy and discolored fedora lent him I don't know what resemblance to the lamps that nobody had bothered to put out and that weakly competed with the pitiless light of morning.

It is possible that, during the first few moments, he made a pretense of not noticing my presence but, upon discovering me standing next to him, lowered his head and extended to me a boneless, weedy hand. I experienced a flutter identical to that produced by unsuspected contact with a glove lying at the bottom of a pocket. I wiped off the moisture with which he had contaminated mine and drew up a chair. It was evident that this disturbed him. As we exchanged our first words, his glances grazed objects in a choppy flight and returned to submerge themselves in his pupils without perturbing the reflection of the lights settled in them, as if in a stagnant puddle. It was urgent to draw him out of that apathy. With the greatest possible cruelty I told him that he looked bad and must surely be very ill. This trick, as expected, succeeded. With one gulp, he polished off the whiskey we had ordered and, letting his arms drop off the table, exclaimed:

"I can't take it anymore! I don't know what to do! I'm desperate!"

Choked, hoarse, his voice seemed to emerge from behind a closed curtain. As if opening it suddenly, he asked me:

"Have you never been tortured by noises? No! I'm sure you haven't. It's so horrible! Horrible!"

The obvious disproportion between the cause and effect of his misery almost made me smile. In any case, it was only then that he looked me in the face, before proceeding in a tone accented by a certain rancor:

"No! I am sure not! You can't understand me. For that, I would have to be like you. You have nothing to grab hold of. I may not count for much, but at least I have this," he went on, extracting a little flask whose filthy label made plain its pharmaceutical contents. "This! For me, it's everything. Nothing else is left. Absolutely nothing."

And, forestalling inferences, he explained:

"It all started with my upstairs neighbor. Night after night I was disturbed by the sound of footsteps above my ceiling. Little by little, their monotonous regularity assumed a stern solemnity! It was like someone knocking on the door of a house where nobody lives. Each time more ponderous, each time closer to my head, I sensed them plunging down from the ceiling, from one end to the other, until I was convinced they would finish me off by pummeling me like hammer-blows.

"I inquired as to who lived in the room above. It turned out to be a student who spent the greater part of the night reading. As the state of my account and my relations with the landlord precluded the possibility of getting assistance from that quarter, I decided to intervene with my neighbor directly. This initiative produced a satisfactory result. For several days, the rafters remained still. Once in a while a slam or a shout rose from the stairwell, but these noises were intermittent: they let me rest. Between one noise and the next there were great gaps of silence and of happiness.

"In a short time, however, all my neighbor's precautions turned into a regime of persecution more torturous than before. Stretched out on my bed, I saw him, for hours at a time, pace from one side of his room to the other, as if the floorboards were translucent. The care with which he opened a drawer, or placed his pipe on his desk, came to agitate me to the point where I had to bury my head in my pillow in order to drown out a yowl of impatience. I believed that he was deliberately engineering ways to prolong my agony, and I attributed every unexpected or improvident disturbance, however small, to his invention. The most treacherous dangled, like spiders, from the rafters and made the pile of the carpet stand on end, then reproduced themselves in the corners, behind the clothes closet, underneath the bed. So high was my state of excitement that it was not long before I was able to perceive, from my fifth floor quarters, simultaneously and with the most pronounced acuity, the conversations of the people who passed along the sidewalk, the purl of the faucet in the patio downstairs, the snores from every room in the building. Although by now I had been spying on them for weeks at a time and ended up knowing the schedules and routines of the majority of these noises, there was always something impossible to locate except inside my head. It was worse plunging myself under the blankets! In direct ratio as those on the outside were lulled and fell asleep, those dwelling in my interior began to awake, one by one, and, not content with gnashing their teeth like newborn mice, scrambled around in my stomach until they wracked me with throes so severe that, as absurd as it seems, I believed I was on the verge of giving birth to a child.

"One exasperating night I decided to go out into the street. I foresaw what awaited me, the effect that would be produced in me by the clatter of the traffic, but anything was preferable to staying in my room. At the corner, I took the first streetcar to pass by. What happened next I can't describe. One moment I felt fine, and the next I felt as if my head were splitting into pieces, but the intensity of the pain engrossed me in such a deep insensibility that when the streetcar stopped to undertake its return trip I was surprised to find myself in the suburbs.

"European capitals lack precise boundaries, they amalgamate and confuse themselves with the towns surrounding them. Buenos Aires, on the other hand, in certain districts at least, terminates brusquely, without preamble. Some scattered houses, like dice on green velvet, and suddenly: the countryside, a countryside as authentic as you please. It's as if the outskirts cannot bring themselves to go far from the cobblestones. And if a shop or market should run this risk, it does so by fronting on the pampas. At night, above all, you have only to walk a few blocks in the outskirts to find yourself unaccompanied by lights. Of the metropolis nothing remains but a blushing sky.

"Only a few minutes from the spot where I got off the streetcar later I found myself in the open country. Never had I experienced such an abundance! My brain was becoming saturated, as if it were a sponge, by an elemental and maritime silence: savoring the night, I fed upon it, I nibbled away, minus condiments, *au naturel;* delightedly picking out its lettucelike flavors, its plush carnosity, the piquant torpor of its stars.

"I'd been influenced, probably, by the anguish of the preceding days. However it happened, this instant alone was sufficient to give me a reason for living and to justify my existence. One has to have undergone the direst moments before he can feel something comparable."

Since the derogatory intent of this last remark was evident, I did not want to interrupt him.

"From that day on," he added, now without boasting, "I adhered to the same itinerary every night. The succeeding ones, nevertheless, were not so fortunate. I looked with loathing at the rough tread of my steps on the earth and was disgusted by the obstinacy with which the insects bored into the silence. I was convinced that the chirping of the crickets possessed an aggressive intention and, what was much more as ignominious, that the toads were laughing at me.

"In spite of all this, for a month and a half I kept up these excursions. Anything was preferable to putting up with the echo cham-

ber into which my room had been transformed. A few days later there transpired,
however, an event that obliged me to give
them up forever.

"It was a magnificent night," he continued,
in a voice still more grating and strained. "As
soon as I got away from the city I noticed that
no noise bothered me. At first I was afraid
that I'd gone deaf. On the contrary. I could
hear with extraordinary clarity, but without
pain or discomfort. I don't know how many
blocks I wandered in the intoxication and the
relief of this verification. At one point, my
legs refused to take another step. I searched
for a spot where I could rest and lean back on
my elbows alongside the roadway.

"Nowhere is the sky so rich in constellations. While we are contemplating it this way,
everything else almost disappears and in a
short while we become so completely absorbed in it that we lose all contact with the
earth. It's as if we are reclining on the deck of
a bobbing boat, gazing at waters so serene
that they immobilize the reflection of the
stars.

"Immersed in this contemplation, I had completely forgotten myself when suddenly a mellow voice pronounced my name. Although I was sure I was alone, the voice was so clear that I straightened up to investigate. Along both sides of the road, the countryside stretched away without interruption. One tree after another was lost in the immensity, but nearby there was a tangle of thistles from among which emerged a bulk that turned out to be a cow grazing in the pasture.

"I was about to stretch out again but, before a minute passed, heard the voice say to me:

'Have you no shame? Is it possible? What has brought you to this state? So now you can't even live among people?'

"As absurd as it may seem, I couldn't escape the conclusion that the voice originated at the place where I had encountered the cow. With the utmost discretion, I turned around to observe it. The clarity of the night permitted me to distinguish its every move. After stirring itself and taking a few steps, it paused a couple of yards from where I stood and, while chewing its cud, continued in an afflicted tone:

'You could have been so happy! You are refined, intelligent and egoistic. But what have you done with your life? Deceived, deceived...nothing but deceived! And now it turns out the same old way: you are the only one who is deceived. You make me want to cry! Ever since you were a boy you have always been so proud! You consider yourself to be above everyone and everything. Above reproach. You believe you have been living more intensely than anyone else. But, would you dare to deny it? You have never given of yourself. When I think how you would prefer anything to actually finding yourself! How is it possible that you can live with such emptiness? Why do you persist in filling it with nothing?

'You are incapable of holding out your hand, of opening your arms. It's truly depressing! It makes me want to cry!'

"When she shut up, I got up quietly without thinking and took a few steps towards her. She gazed at me tenderly with her moist, limpid eyes and rubbed her muzzle against a fencepost. Then she stuck her neck through the barbed wire and puckered her lips to kiss me.

"Motionless, separated only by a narrow ditch, we stared at one another in silence. I could have dropped to my knees, but I gave a leap and broke into a run down the road. In the depths of my being swelled the certainty that the voice I had just heard was that of my mother."

There was so much emotion packed into the last part of the story that I didn't dare crack a smile. And, as his confidence grew, he added, after a silence:

"And the worst thing is that my mother, the cow, is right. I have never been anything but a cork. All my life long I have floated from here to there, without knowing anything but the surface of things. Incapable of attaching myself to anything or anyone, I have always drifted away from others before I could learn to love them. And now it's too late. I lack the courage to put on my slippers."

As if resonating inside an unfurnished

room, his voice was marked by an inflection so cavernous that I reflexively scoured the surroundings for some gesture or facial expression that might accompany it. But I found myself completely alone. Between his forlornity and my silence was interposed a cloud that grew denser by the moment. There was nothing left to do but wait and see if the morning would dissipate it.

It wasn't long before the slippery hour of dawn elapsed and brought on that instant in which things change consistency and size, so as to ground themselves, definitively, in reality. Perched on one foot, the trees shook off their dreams and their sparrows, while from street to street the asphalt lost its sheen of undeveloped film. With a metallic yawn, businesses reopened their doors and relit their showcases. On the sidewalks, in the recently awakened entryways, noises acquired an adolescent sonority. From time to time, a somnolent car transported a lump of countryside to the city and, from all around us, wafted the odor of warm bread and of ink still wet from the press.

Side by side, we strolled along without saying a word. Head hunched between his shoulders, his walk wobbly and somnambular, he would not have surprised me if he had collapsed on somebody's doorstep, the way his garments looked as if they might suddenly drop to the ground, as if slipping from a clothes-rack. His fedora, his overcoat, his trousers seemed so limp and baggy that for a moment I resisted admitting that those were his steps resounding on the sidewalk. While we were passing in front of a dairy, an old woman spied on us with myopic distrust; almost at the same time, a dog stopped to stare with the same insistence, so that my companion quickened his pace for fear that it would draw nearer and confuse him with a tree. I surmised that his shadow, being too heavy and too dense, had neglected to follow him. Was it repulsed by living with him, constantly suffering his presence? It occurred to me that some night, while crossing the street and rounding a corner, he would be left to go on alone forever. When we came to the front door of the rooming house, I capitulated to the heartlessness of custom and bid him farewell.

After that, I never saw him again. A while back, I ascertained that, upon returning to Paris, he published, with success, a book of poetry. Recently someone informed me that the Russian secret service had made him face a firing squad after sending him on a mission to China.

Which of these stories is true? I don't think anyone can say for sure. It may be that by now there is nothing left of his person but a lock of hair and a set of false teeth. It's very possible that, pursued by the fear of falling asleep, he can be found at these hours in some café, beset by the same weariness as always...with a few flakes of dandruff on his shoulders and the smile of an empty, worn-out wallet.

This last is the most probable. His mother, the cow, knew that well enough.

"Lunarlude" was reprinted from *Scarecrow and Other Anomalies* (Riverside, California: Xenos Books, 2002), translated by Gilbert Alter-Gilbert. ©2002 by Gilbert Alter-Gilbert. Reprinted by permission of Xenos Books and the translator.

Hagiwara Sakutarō (Japan)

 *Born into a wealthy family, Hagiwara Sakutarō (1886-1942) was able as a young man to devote himself to po-etry. Although he did not fin-ish college, he read Western authors, including Poe, Niet-zsche, Schopenhauer, and Dostoevsky. His major works of poetry, written in 1917 and 1923, were* Howling at the Moon *and* Blue, *both published in a translated edition by Green Integer. These works, as well as his prose-poem* roman *"Cat Town," transformed modern Japanese poetry, and changed forever the face of the future poetic landscape in Japan.*

Cat Town

—*Roman* in the style of a Prose Poem—

You may smash a fly but the fly's "thing in itself" will not die. You'd simply have smashed the phenomenon called a fly.

—SCHOPENHAUER

I

The allure of travel gradually faded away from my romantic fantasy. Once upon a time my heart used to dance just by imagining any of their symbols, such as a train, a steamship, towns of an unknown foreign land. But my past experiences have taught me that traveling is no more than a simple "movement of the same thing within the same space." No matter where you go, you find the same kinds of people living in the same kinds of villages or towns repeating the same kinds of monotonous lives. In any small town in the countryside, merchants are fiddling with their abacuses in their stores, looking out at the whitish street all day, public servants are smoking in their offices, thinking about things like the vegetables in their lunch boxes, as they live through each tasteless, monotonous day the same way, day after day, watching their lives gradually grow old. The allure of travel came merely to project in my exhausted heart an endlessly bored landscape like a Chinese parasol that grows in some vacant lot, making me feel a tasteless hatred for human life in which identical rules repeat themselves no matter where you turn. In short, I lost interest and romance in any kind of travel.

For quite a long time I continued mysterious travels through my own unique method. In these travels of mine I let myself go in the only moments where human beings can fly outside time and space, outside cause and effect, that is, that free world that subjectivity constructs, skillfully taking advantage of the borderlines between dreams and reality. This said, I no longer will need to talk a lot about my secret. Only, I'd just add that in my case, instead of opium which requires you to go to a great deal of trouble for utensils and equipment and which in Japan is hard to get, I most often used morphine and cocaine, which you can use by simple injection or orally. As for the countries I traveled in the dreams induced by narcotics, I don't have enough room to detail them here. But in most cases I traveled in marshy areas swarming with frogs or a coastal region, near the Pole, where penguins are. In the landscapes of those dreams, all colors were in brilliant primary hues, and both the sea and the sky were transparently blue like glass. Even after I woke from them, I retained these visions in my memory, often experiencing eerie hallucinations in the real world.

These travels on drugs, however, terribly harmed my health. Every day I became exhausted, turned paler, and my skin grew old and stagnant. I began to pay attention to my own care. And in the midst of a walk for exercise, one day suddenly I discovered a new method of satisfying my oddball travel addiction. Following the advice my doctor specified for me, every day I walked about in an area four to five thousand yards away from home (for thirty minutes to an hour). That day, too, I was, as always, walking in the usual walking area. The route I took was always the same. But that day I, for some reason, passed through an alley unknown to me. As a result,

170   1001 Great Stories

I completely lost track of my route, messing up the direction. From the beginning I've been a human being whose sensory functions that intuit magnetic directions have something remarkably deficient about them. In consequence, I don't remember roads well, and in a place unfamiliar to any extent I easily get lost. In addition, I have the habit of falling into meditation while walking on the road. An acquaintance may greet me without my noticing it at all; at times I become lost in my neighborhood, very near my house, and ask for directions, making people laugh. Once I walked around the house where I'd lived for a long time, round and round along the fence fifty, sixty times. Because of the error in my directional sense I could not for the life of me find the entrance to the gate that was right in front of my eyes. My family said I was no doubt duped by a fox. The state of being duped by a fox must be what the psychologist calls disorder in the semicircular canals. This is because, according to scholars' theory, the special function of sensing directions resides in them.

Such extraneous matters aside, I was lost and confused; making a wild guess, I hurried along the road, trying to go in the direction of my house. And after making several rounds of a suburban area with mansions with many trees, I suddenly came out on a bustling street. It was a beautiful town in some place utterly unknown to me. The street was swept into cleanliness and the pavement was wet with dew. Every store was neat and clean, and each show window with a polished plate glass had a variety of rare merchandise arranged in it. Near the eaves of a café a flowering tree luxuriated, adding a touch of light and shadow to the town. The red mailbox at the crossroads was also beautiful, and even the young woman in the cigarette store was bright and lovely like an apricot. I had never seen a town with such deep feeling. Where on earth in Tokyo was such a town? I had forgotten the geography. But from a time computation, I knew for certain, without any doubt, that it was in the neighborhood of my house, that it was in the usual area for my walk, only about thirty minutes away on foot, or somewhere near it. But how was it possible that such a town existed so close, utterly unknown to me?

I felt I was dreaming. It seemed to me it was not a real town, but a town in a picture projected on a screen for a magic lantern. At that instant, however, my memory and common sense were recovered. I looked again, and it was a suburban town near my place that I knew very well, unattractive and ordinary. As always, the mailbox stood at the crossroads, and in the cigarette store a young woman with a stomach ailment was sitting. And in the show windows of the stores was the usual merchandise on display that had gone out of fashion, yawning in a dusty manner. The eaves of the café were decorated with an arch of artificial flowers quite appropriate for the countryside. It was no more than the usual, boring town in which everything was just as I knew it. In a single instant the entire impression had changed. And this magical, mysterious change was caused by the simple fact that I had become lost on my way and had hallucinated about the direction.

The mailbox which usually was at the southern edge of the town seemed to be in the north, at the entrance from the opposite end. The houses lining the street, which were usually on the left side, had moved to the opposite, right side. And this simple change had made the entire town appear a rarity, something new.

In that unknown, hallucinatory town I was looking at the sign of a certain store. I thought I'd seen exactly the same picture somewhere. And the moment my memory was restored, all directions were reversed. The street that until then had been on the left side was on the right side, I discovered, and I, who had been walking north, was walking south. That instant, the needle on the magnetic compass turned round, and the spatial positions of east, west, south, and north were entirely reversed. At the same time, the entire universe changed, the feelings of the phenomenal town became something utterly different. That is, the mysterious town I'd seen before had actually existed in the reverse space of the universe where the magnetic compass was turned upside down.

After this accidental discovery, I often deliberately got directions wrong to travel in this mysterious space. These travels were also convenient for my purpose because of the deficiency I've described before. But even those with an ordinary, healthy directional sense must see, from time to time, this special space in their own experiences. For example, you take a train late at night to go home. When it leaves the station, the train at first runs on the rail straight from east to west. After a while, you wake from your dozing dreams. And you begin to realize that the direction of the advancing train had been reversed before you knew it, with the train running in the opposite direction, from west to east. In your rational thinking, you know it isn't possible. Yet as a sensory fact, the train is certainly going the other way, away from your destination. At such a time, look out the window. The stations and landscapes on the way that are so familiar to you have now entirely, fascinatingly changed, presenting an utterly different world of which you don't have a fragment of memory. But when you finally reach your destination and get off on the usual platform, you for the first time wake from your dream and recognize the real, correct direction. And once you realize this, the abnormal landscapes and things you saw turn into unattractive, ordinary, familiar, and banal things. That is, you see the same landscape first from its reverse side, then from its front according to normal custom. Nothing contains a greater metaphysical mystery than the fact that a single thing presents two separate sides if you change the direction of your eyes, that a single phenomenon has a hidden "secret side." Long ago, when I was a child, I would look at a picture hung on the wall and become obsessed with the thought: What kind of world is secretly hidden behind the framed landscape painting? I often removed the oil painting to peer at its back. This question I had as a child remains to me, an adult today, as an unsolvable mystery.

The story I narrate next provides a key that suggests an answer to my mystery. If the reader is able to hypothesize from my myste-

rious tale a certain four-dimensional world—
the reality behind the landscape—that hides
behind things and phenomena, the entire tale
will be real. But if you are unable to hypothesize it, the facts that I actually experienced
will after all be no more than a hallucination
of incoherent decadence of a poet whose cen-
tral nerves have been damaged by morphine
addiction. At any rate, I'll muster the courage
to write it down. However, not being a novelist, I don't know how to amuse the reader
with embellishment and schema. All I can do
will be to write a report on the facts I experienced.

2

At the time I was staying at a hot-springs site
called K in the Hokuetsu region. In the mountains near the end of September, and past the
seven autumn equinox days, it was already
deeply autumnal. All the resort people from

the metropolis had gone back, with only a handful of people seeking a hot-spring cure quietly staying on to look after their illnesses. The sun was casting a deeper shadow, and in the desolate courtyard of the inn were dead leaves of trees scattered about. In a flannel kimono I would take a walk in the mountain at the back as part of the assignment of days with nothing to do.

A little distance away from my hot spring there were three small towns. They were not so much towns as small congregations of farmhouses more properly called villages, but one of them was really a compact rural town selling an array of daily necessities, with even a couple of urban-style restaurants. From the hot spring a straight road led to each of these towns, and every day a horse carriage traveled back and forth on a set schedule. Also, to the most town-like town, called U, there was a light railway. I often took it to go there, to do shopping or drink at a restaurant provided with a barmaid. But my true joy was on the way to the town. The cute, toy-like train ran, twisting and turning through deciduous woods and between mountains with a view of a valley.

One day I got off the train midway to walk to U Town. I wanted to take a leisurely walk all by myself over a mountain pass which had a good view. The road lay more or less alongside the railway as it followed an irregular path through the woods. Here and there autumn grasses bloomed, there was clay exposing its shiny flesh, and there were trees cut and laid down. Looking at the clouds floating in the sky, I was thinking of the old folklore transmitted in that mountainous region. The region, which was on the whole culturally undeveloped and enveloped with taboos and superstitions of a primitive people, had in fact a variety of legends and folklore in which many people there still seriously believed. Indeed, the maids at my inn, as well as the people from neighboring villages who were taking a hot-spring cure, told me various stories with feelings of fear and disgust. According to what they said, the residents of one village were possessed by a dog deity and the residents of another by a cat deity. Those possessed by a dog deity ate only meat, and those possessed by a cat deity only fish, to survive.*

These people called such outlandish villages "possessed villages" and avoided all intercourse with them, hating and detesting them. The people of "possessed villages" choose a dark, moonless night once every month to hold a rite. The rite is utterly invisible except to themselves. On a rare occasion some outsider might see it, but such a person, for some reason, keeps mum about it. They have a unique magical power and have a huge amount of assets, source unknown, stashed away somewhere. And so forth.

After telling me such stories, they would add: In fact, a village of that kind existed near this hot spring until just recently. Its residents have scattered away someplace now, you can guess why, but they must be continuing their secret group life. For an unmistakable proof

---

* Based on a common observation in Japan that cats show a marked preference for fish.

of this, we know someone who saw their Okura (the true identify of the evil deity). In the talks of these people, there was a strain of stubborn assertiveness unique to the farmers. Regardless of my wishes, they tried to impose on me their own superstitious fear and its reality. But I had a different reason to listen to their stories with fascination. Village taboos of this kind, which are found in many parts of Japan, can probably be linked to the descendants of the people who had as their tribal deities those who had moved here from foreign countries or had naturalized and whose customs and habits were different. Or, to make a more credible guess, they may be linked to the villages of "hiding Christians." But in this universe there are a great many things that are unknown to mankind. As Horace said, intellect knows nothing. It turns everything into common sense and provides vulgar interpretations to mythologies. And the hidden meaning of the universe is always above vulgarity. Therefore, all philosophers must yield to the poet at the ultimate end of their reasoning. Only the universe that the poet intuits far above the common senses is the true metaphysical reality.

Deep in such thought, I was walking along the autumn mountain path. The narrow path went on to lead into the depths of the woods. The railway that I had counted on as the only road sign to my destination was nowhere visible. I had lost track of my way.

"Lost!"

What came to my mind when I awoke from meditation was this helpless word. I suddenly became uneasy and hurriedly started to look for the path. I turned back and tried to return to the original road. In that attempt I lost my sense of geography and found myself mired in a labyrinth which seemed to lead every which way. The mountain became deeper, and the small path disappeared into thorns. Useless time passed. I didn't even meet a single woodcutter. My unease increased. As agitated as a dog, I walked about trying to sniff out the road. And finally I found a narrow path which had clear footprints of men and horses. Paying attention to those footprints, I gradually descended toward the foot of the mountain. No matter to which side of the mountain I might go down, I'd be relieved as long as I could get to a place with houses.

Some hours later I reached the foot of the mountain. And, totally unexpectedly, I discovered a human world I hadn't thought of. There, instead of poor farmhouses, was a beautiful, bustling town. Once, an acquaintance of mine, who had traveled on the Siberian Railway, told me how, after running through the vast, barren, uninhabited plain on the train day after day after day, the small station where the train stopped at long last looked like the busiest city in the world. My impression in this case was a comparable surprise. Toward the lower flatland spread innumerable houses of different designs, with towers and tall buildings shining in the sun. I could hardly believe that such a gigantic city existed in such a god-forsaken mountain.

Feeling as if I were watching a magic lantern, I slowly approached the town. And in the end I went into the lantern myself. Out of a certain narrow alley, I passed through a street as in a prenatal labyrinth unto the center of a bustling boulevard. My impression of the city streets I saw with my eyes was very special and rare. In each block the stores and buildings were designed with artistically different feelings, yet the town as a whole formed a comprehensive beauty. Furthermore, it was not consciously done but was an accidental result after rust gathered for ages. It had ancient elegance and depth and spoke of the town's history of a long past and its residents' long memories. The streets were generally narrow, even the boulevard only four or five yards wide at best. The smaller streets were jammed between the eaves, forming narrow, crisscrossing alleys. They turned and twisted like a labyrinth, sometimes going down a pavement, sometimes going through a dark tunnel that formed under bay windows that jutted out on the second floors. As in a town in a southern land, luxurious flowering trees grew here and there, with wells near them. Everywhere the shadow was deep, and the town as a whole had the moist quietude of the shade of green foliage. There was a line of houses that looked like brothels, and from somewhere deep in the courtyard came the sound of quiet, leisurely music.

Along the boulevard many houses were Western-style, with glass windows. At the eaves of a barbershop a pole with red and white stripes stuck out and written on its painted sign was *Barbershop*. There was an inn, and there was a cleaner. At the crossroads of the town was a photo studio, and its glass-made house like a weather station reflected the blue sky of an autumn day in a somewhat lonesome fashion. At the front end of a clock-and-watch store sat its bespectacled proprietor doing his work silently, intently.

The town was bustling with people thronging the streets. And yet there was no noise whatever; it was all elegantly quiet, forlorn, and hushed, as it cast a shadow like deep sleep. This was because, except for the people who were walking, not a single car or horse that made noise passed by. Not only that, the crowds themselves were quiet. Both men and women all appeared refined and reserved, cultivated and unhurried. In particular, the women were beautiful; in addition to being ladylike, they were coquettish. Whether shopping in a store or gossiping on a street, they were all well-mannered, speaking in a harmonious, low, quiet voice. Their talking and conversation had the air of not so much listening with the ear as manually exploring the meaning with some sort of feeler. In particular, the women's voices had the sweet entrancing charm of caressing the surface of the skin. All the phenomena and personalities went back and forth like shadows.

The first thing I noticed was that the atmosphere of this town as a whole was formed artificially with terribly delicate attentiveness. The entire nervous system of not simply the buildings but also the mood of the town was focused solely on a certain important aesthetic design. Attention was given to every corner lest the slightest stirring of the air break any of the rules for beauty, such as contrast, balance, harmony, and parallelism. Furthermore, because the formation of the rules for beauty required a terribly complicated differential calculation, every nerve of the town was quivering with extraordinary tension. For example, even a high-pitched voice out of tune in the slightest was prohibited because it would break the harmony. Whether walking on the street, simply moving a hand, eating or drinking something, contemplating, or selecting the design of a kimono, *delicate* attention always had to be given to keep in harmony with the atmosphere of the town, not to destroy the contrast and balance with the surroundings. The entire town was like a dangerous, fragile building formed of a thin sheet of glass. The slightest loss of balance would destroy the whole house, shattering the glass into smithereens. The maintenance of its stability required each of its columns to be assembled with delicate mathematical logic, the whole structure being supported, barely, by the resultant contrast and balance. What was frightening was that was the reality and the fact of the town's structure. A single careless mistake would mean its collapse and death. The nerves of the entire town were tense with that apprehension and terror. The design of the town that seemed aesthetic was not for simple tastefulness but hid a terrifyingly acute problem.

When I noticed this, I suddenly became uneasy and felt the pain of my nerves tensing up in the electrifying air that surrounded me. Now both the unique beauty of the town and its hushed, dreamy quietness became eerie in a hushed sort of way as if signals were being exchanged inside some frightening secret. A single unknown, vague presentiment busily ran about in my heart, in a pale terrifying color. All my senses were liberated, and I could perceive completely, surely, the minutest colors, smells, sounds, tastes, and even the meanings of things. The air surrounding me filled with an odor like that of a corpse, and the atmospheric pressure kept climbing by the second. What phenomenized there was surely some evil omen. Surely now, something extraordinary would happen! Had to happen!

The town hadn't changed a bit. The streets were as thronged as before, refined people walking quietly, noiselessly. Somewhere in the distance there were consecutive low sorrowful sounds like the rasping of a Chinese fiddle. Mine was a presentiment whose content was terrible anxiety, like that of someone who, in some place, alone, mystified and suspicious, is watching a town which, just a moment before a great earthquake strikes, remains as normal as normal can be. Now, accidentally, a man falls. And the carefully constructed harmony is destroyed, throwing the entire town into chaos.

In my own presentiment I became exasperated like someone who, conscious that he is dreaming his nightmare, is desperately writhing in his effort to wake from it. The sky was transparently blue and clear, and the density of the electrified air kept increasing even faster. The buildings began to become uneasily distorted, turning emaciated as if ill. Here and there, tower-like things became visible. The roofs, too, became eerily slender, looking oddly bony and deformed like the legs of a skinny chicken.

"Now!"

When I shouted despite myself, my heart pounding with terror, a tiny, black, rat-like animal scurried away through the center of town. In my eyes it made a truly clear image. For some reason I had an abnormal, abrupt impression of something that threatened to break the entire harmony.

That instant. All phenomena came to a sudden halt, and a bottomless silence laid itself down. I didn't know what it was. But the next instant, a frightening abnormality, which no one could imagine and which was the most bizarre in the world, phenomenized. I looked and the streets of the town were swarming with huge crowds of cats. Cat, cat, cat, cat, cat, cat, cat. No matter where I looked, there were only cats. And from the windows of houses cats' whiskered faces were floating out, enlarged, as if they were pictures in picture frames.

I shuddered, my breathing almost stopped, I was about to faint and keel over. Is this not a world where human beings live but a town where only cats live? What on earth has happened? How can I believe this phenomenon? I'm sure something is wrong with my brain now. I am seeing an illusion. Or else I've gone mad. My own universe has lost its conscious balance and collapsed.

I became afraid of myself. I strongly felt some frightening final destruction was pressing very close upon me. A shudder flashed through the darkness. But the next moment I recovered my consciousness. Quietly calming myself down, I opened my eyes once again and looked again at the truth of the fact. By then all those enigmatic cats had vanished from my vision. There was nothing abnormal about the town, and the windows were open, *vacant.* There was nothing in the streets, only the roads of boredom whitening. Nothing like cats were visible anywhere. And the emotional state had completely changed. Banal commercial houses lined the town, and tired dusty people of the kind you'd see in any countryside were walking in the dry daytime town. The mesmerizing mysterious town had wholly disappeared and as if you'd turned over a card, a completely different world had emerged. What actualized itself here was the usual banal rural town. Furthermore, it was the usual U Town that I'd known so well.

There the usual barbershop, with its chairs lined up for customers who didn't come, was watching the daytime street, and on the left side of the rundown town the clock-and-watch store that couldn't sell its wares was yawning, its door closed as usual. Altogether it was a monotonous town in the countryside just as I'd known it, with nothing unusual about it.

When my consciousness had become that clear, I understood everything. Stupid of me, I had once again suffered the usual sensory disease, "the loss of semicircular canals." I had lost my ideas of directions ever since I was lost on the path in the mountain. I thought I had gone down the opposite side, but had come back down to U Town. And I had wandered into the center of town from a direction totally different from the station where I normally got off the train. As a result, I had looked at all the impressions from the opposite side, from a position where the magnetic compass was flipped upside down, and had seen another, four-dimensional universe (the other side of the landscape) where the upside

192   1001 Great Stories

and downside, the four directions, the front and back, and the right and left were all reversed. That is, to provide an interpretation from the run-of-the-mill kind of common sense, I had been "duped by a fox," as they say.

3

My story ends here. But my mysterious question begins anew here. The Chinese philosopher Chuang Tzu once turned into a butterfly in his dream and when he awoke from it asked, mystified: Am I the butterfly in the dream or am I the one who dreamed it? This ancient enigma hasn't been solved by anyone for thousands of years. Is a hallucinated universe what someone duped by a fox sees? Or does commonsensical intellect see it? In the first place, does the metaphysical real world exist on the other side or this side of the landscape? Probably no one can give an answer to this enigma. And yet what still remains in my memory is that puzzling non-human town, that spectacle of a monstrous cat town in which vivid images of cats were projected in the windows, under the eaves, and on the streets. My living sensory ability can still recreate that frightening impression and make me see it vividly, right in front of my eyes, even though fifteen to sixteen years have already passed.

People sneer at my story, saying that it's a poet's sickly hallucination, just a silly phantasmagoric illusion. Yet I surely saw a town where only cats lived, a town where cats in the guise of human beings thronged its streets. Regardless of any ratiocination or argument, to me nothing is more absolute and doubtless than the fact that I saw it in some part of the universe. Despite all the kinds of jeering of all those many people, I still firmly believe in my mind the villages on the Japan Sea which oral legend has handed down, and that the town in which only feline spirits live must surely exist in some part of the universe.

Reprinted from *Howling at the Moon: Poems and Prose of Hagiwara Sakutarō* (Los Angeles: Green Integer, 2002), translated from the Japanese by Hiroaki Sato. ©2002 by Hiroaki Sato. Reprinted by permission of Green Integer.

Georg Heym (Germany)

The son of a Prussian military lawyer, Georg Heym (1887-1912) rebelled against his conservative family to become one of the outstanding poets of the Expressionist generation in Germany. His first volume of poetry, De ewige Tag, *was published in 1911 to great acclaim. One critic likened him to Arthur Rimbaud and named him the outstanding young poet in Germany. In January 1912 Heym was drowned when he fell through the ice while skating on the Havel river in Berlin. "An Afternoon: Contribution to the History of a Little Boy" was first published in 1913 as* Der Dieb. Ein Novellenbuch.

An Afternoon

Contribution to the History of a Little Boy

The street looked to him like a long pencil-stroke, with passers-by who were no more than inflated white dolls. They couldn't know about his happiness, could they? He had asked her, "May I kiss you?" this little boy, and she had held out her lips and he had kissed them. And this kiss burnt deeply into his heart, like a big pure flame, which released him, made him happy, made him blissful. Ye Gods, he would like to have danced with happiness. And the sky ran away above him like a great blue road; the light traveled westwards like a fiery wagon, and all the glowing houses seemed to reflect the blaze.

He felt as if his life were thunderously large, as though he had never lived so much before, as if he were swimming high in the air like a bird, sunk in the eternal ether, boundlessly free, boundlessly happy, boundlessly alone.

And the invisible crown of happiness lay

on his square childish forehead and beauti-
fied it, like a night landscape lit by multiple
flashes of lightning.

"Ye Gods! I'm loved! I'm loved! What it is
to be loved so much!" He went faster, broke
into a run, as though his usual measured gait
were too slow for the storm rushing in his
heart. In this state he ran down the street and
sat by the sea.

"Oh sea, sea!" and he told his experience to
the sea, in a brief shout of joy, a trembling
whisper, a flurry of silent speech. And the sea
understood him and listened to him, the sea,
over whose blue droning expanse the hurri-
cane of joy and the sobs of grief had reverber-
ated for so many millennia, like a perpetual
whirlwind over an eternally untouched deep.

He preserved his loneliness nervously.
When people came he sprang up, ran away
and crept into the dunes. Once they had gone
by, he ran forward again to the sea, whose
enormous expanse was the only cup into
which he could pour the flood of his endless
excess.

Gradually the beach grew livelier. White

dresses were flashing all over the place be-tween the basket-chairs, old ladies came with books under their arms. Bright sunshades bobbed on the narrow wooden walkways, and crowds of children filled up the sand-castles again. Rowing-boats put out to sea, sails were hoisted on the big yachts, a photographer waded through the sand with his camera on a strap over his shoulder.

He looked at the time. A half an hour more, twenty-nine minutes, then he'll be meeting her. He will take her by the hand, they will go together into the wood, where it's perfectly quiet. And there they will sit down together, hand in hand, hidden in the green thicket.

But what will he say, to stop her thinking he's boring? Because she's like a little lady al-ready, you have to entertain her, make jokes.

Whatever should he say to her?

Oh, he won't speak at all, and she'll under-stand him that way too. They will look into each other's eyes, and their eyes will say quite enough.

And then she will hold out her mouth to

Georg Heym/ An Afternoon

him again, he will take her head lightly in his arm, like this, like this—he tried it on a stalk of broom—and then he will kiss her, very softly, very tenderly.

And they will sit that way, together in the wood, together until dark; oh how lovely, how lovely, what complete bliss.

They will never leave each other. He will work all the time, he will get through his studies quickly, and one day he will marry her. And life seemed to the child like a clear straight road, leading into a sky of endless blue, short, simple, uneventful, like an endless garden.

He stood up and went over the beach through the playing children, the people, and the basket-chairs. A steamer came in, a stream of people swelled towards the landing-stage. A bell was rung. He saw none of it; the things which would previously have riveted his attention had disappeared. His eyes were directed inwards, as though he needed all his time to study the new person that had suddenly emerged from the locked core of his being.

He came to the bench where he was to meet his little girlfriend; she was not yet there.

But of course it was still too early. There were still ten minutes to go. She probably had to have coffee before leaving; her mother wouldn't have let her go yet.

He sat for a few minutes on the bench, then stood up again and ran back and forth a few times in the little circle of trees. Only two minutes left, he should be able to see her by now. He scanned the path for her. But the path stayed empty. Its trees hid nobody. They stood, softly gilded by the afternoon sun, peaceful in the windless air, and through their foliage the light trembled on the path, like on the bed of a golden stream. The treelined walk was like a great, green, quiet hall, with a doorway at the far end, in which there shimmered a small blue stripe, the distant meeting-point of sea and sky.

He trembled. Something contracted inside him. "Why doesn't she come? Why doesn't she come?"

"Ah, isn't that her hat, isn't that the white ribbon? That's her, that's her."

And the door of his soul sprang open, he was shaken by a storm, he ran to meet her. As he came nearer, he saw that he had made a mistake. That wasn't she at all, it was someone else. And that moment he felt something being stifled in him, as though he was being strangled.

He had a familiar feeling suddenly: like once when they were taking him out of a house where there was a dead person and he had stood by the bedside: a sort of disgust, or self-loathing. This particular, strange feeling always came over him when something unpleasant was approaching which he could not get out of; mathematics homework, a telling-off.

But he had never felt it so strongly before. He could almost taste it on his tongue, bitter, like something grey.

His blood seemed to stand still; it was uncanny to be so inert. His forehead had gone small, and grey, as though someone had overshadowed it with his hand.

He went back slowly to the circle under the tree. "But she'll come, of course she will." Of course she could be late. If only she would come! She could be a quarter of an hour late as far as he was concerned, just so long as she finally came.

He looked at his watch again. The time had gone by, and the second hand ran ever further ahead like a small thin spider in a silver cage. Its little foot trod on the seconds, which fell away in little jerks, like dust on a tiny country road.

Now four minutes had gone by already, now five. And the minute hand climbed even higher up its little stair. He wanted to go and meet her. But what if she came from another direction? He hesitated; should he stay, should he go? But his unrest drove him out. He ran back a few steps down the path, then he stopped again, and again turned back.

He sat down on the bench, and stared ahead of him. And with every minute his confidence diminished. He would wait till five o'clock; she could still come.

From the distance you might have taken him for an old man from the way he was sitting. Bent, sunk into himself like someone over whom many years of grief have rolled.

He stood up again, and went slowly a few more steps over the scene of his childish tragedy.

In the distance he heard a clock striking, but it was fast. He compared it with his pocket watch. That one was certainly striking too soon. There were still three minutes to five.

And in these three minutes hope reared up once again in his heart: a feeling of longing, like the dying flame from a sinking ember, or like the salute to life in the last heartbeat of a dying person.

Now, now it was time. Now all the towers in the town behind the wood were striking. He saw a bell swinging in the clear air, up in the belfry of a church tower. And at every droning stroke, he felt that his heart was being tugged out of his breast, a little way at a time to make the pain last longer. One tug, another, soon it will be right out, he thought.

The towers went silent; it was quiet again. And in his breast it went quite empty, it was as if there were a great empty hole, as though he were carrying around a dead thing inside.

It felt as though something stupefying had been poured into his blood. It made his head so heavy, it made him so tired.

Over a sunny pond that shimmered through the trees of the public gardens a few puffs of cloud emerged from the chimney of the swimming baths. They flew away in the wind. He watched without interest as they dissolved in the light. Two voices became audible behind the bushes. A pair of nursemaids came along pushing prams.

They settled opposite him on the bench in the circle and lifted the children out of the prams, who straight away tumbled down a heap of sand.

Then he stood up and went away, slowly, his mind a blank.

He came down onto the beach again. He went through the basket-chairs again. The old ladies were still sitting there with their books, the photographer was there, standing in front of a group of people. He must have made a joke, for all of them had laughing faces.

He was carried by the force of his passion towards the basket-chair in which he had received the kiss at midday, like a little ship driven pitilessly by the storm towards a rock.

Perhaps she was still sitting in it. That was his last hope. He slid cautiously between the basket-chairs, nearer and nearer. And the red pennant on top seemed to wave to him.

Now he was very near. He was halted by a vague fear. Then he heard her voice. She was laughing. And now another voice: a boy's.

He crept warily forwards, taking a circuitous route. He dropped into the sand and advanced on all fours. When he was near enough to see them he lay down behind a heap of sand and raised his head slightly over the top.

She was sitting on a boy's lap. The boy pulled her head down to kiss her, then as he released it his hand reached for her leg. The hand slid upwards slowly, and she leaned back, right back, against his shoulder.

The little boy withdrew his head and crept

away, putting one leg behind the other, one hand behind the other, mechanically.

He didn't actually feel anything, no pain. no anguish. He had just one wish, to hide, to creep in somewhere and then lie quite still, find himself a little spot somewhere in the lyme-grass.

And when he was far enough away, he got up out of the sand and went.

On the way he saw a schoolfriend, and hid from him behind a tent. His mother came from the right and called him over. He behaved as though he hadn't heard any thing. He began to run, past the basket-chairs, past the people. And as he ran it occurred to him that he had run like this already today, at midday when he was so happy.

Then he was overcome by grief. He got away quickly up the dunes. At the top he threw himself down with his face in the stalks. The lyme-grass nodded over his head like a wood; a pair of dragonfhes hummed through the stalks.

And that was the first time in the boy's life that he drank the cups of rapture and of torment in the same day. So many times afterwards it was to be his lot to suffer the extremes of joy and the depths of grief, like a precious vessel that has to be able to withstand many passages through the fire without cracking.

Reprinted from *The Thief and Other Stories* (London: Libris, 1994), translated from the Germany by Susan Bennett. © 1994 by Libris. Reprinted by permission of Libris and Susan Bennett.

Aldous Huxley (England/USA)

Born in England in 1894, the grandson of the great biologist Thomas Henry Huxley, Aldous Huxley, who at first wanted to become a doctor, ultimately developed into a major novelist and story writer. His early books were harshly satirical novels, Antic Hay *(1923),* Point Counter Point *(1928),* Eyeless in Gaza *(1936), and the futuristic* Brave New World *(1932), among them. In 1937 Huxley settled in Los Angeles, where he gradually became more and more interested in varieties of spiritual perception. Works such as* The Perennial Philosophy, The Doors of Perception, *and* Heaven and Hell *describe mystical experiences and recount his personal experiments with the drug mescalin.*

"Eupompus Gave Splendour to Art by Numbers" appeared in his collection of tales, Limbo, *published in 1920.*

Eupompus Gave Splendour to Art by Numbers

"I have made a discovery," said Emberlin as I entered his room.

"What about ?" I asked.

"A discovery," he replied, "about *Discoveries*." He radiated an unconcealed satisfaction ; the conversation had evidently gone exactly as he had intended it to go. He had made his phrase, and, repeating it lovingly—"A discovery about *Discoveries*"—he smiled benignly at me, enjoying my look of mystification—an expression which, I confess, I had purposely exaggerated in order to give him pleasure. For Emberlin, in many ways so childish, took an especial delight in puzzling and nonplussing his acquaintances ; and these small triumphs, these little "scores" off people afforded him some of his keenest pleasures. I always indulged his weakness when I could, for it was worth while being on Emberlin's good books. To be allowed to listen to his post-prandial conversation was a privilege indeed. Not only was he himself a consummately good talker, but he had also the power of stimulating others to talk well. He was like some subtle wine, intoxicating just to the Meredithian level of tipsiness. In his company you would find yourself lifted to the sphere of nimble and mercurial conceptions; you would suddenly realize that some miracle had occurred, that you were living no longer in a dull world of jumbled things but somewhere above the hotch-potch in a glassily perfect universe of ideas, where all was informed, consistent, symmetrical. And it was Emberlin who, godlike, had the power of creating this new and real world. He built it out of words, this crystal Eden, where no belly-going snake, devourer of quotidian dirt, might ever enter and disturb its harmonies. Since I first knew Emberlin I have come to have a greatly enhanced respect for magic and all the formules of its liturgy. If by words Emberlin can create a new world for me, can make my spirit slough off completely the domination of the old, why should not he or I or anyone, having found the suitable phrases, exert by means of them an influence more vulgarly miraculous upon the world of mere things? Indeed, when I compare Emberlin and the common or garden black magician of commerce, it seems to me that Emberlin is the greater thaumaturge. But let that pass; I am straying from my purpose, which was to give some description of the man as who so confidentially whispered to me that he had made a discovery about *Discoveries.*

In the best sense of the word, then, Emberlin was academic. For us who knew him his rooms were an oasis of aloofness planted secretly in the heart of the desert of London. He exhaled an atmosphere that combined the fantastic speculativeness of the undergraduate with the more mellowed oddity of incredibly wise and antique dons. He was immensely erudite, but in a wholly unencyclopedic way—a mine of irrelevant information, as his enemies said of him. He wrote a certain amount, but, like Mallarmé, avoided publication, deeming it akin to "the offence of exhibitionism." Once, however, in the folly of youth, some dozen years ago, he had published a volume of verses. He spent a good deal of time now in assiduously collecting copies of his book and burning them. There can be but very few left in the world now. My friend Cope had the fortune to pick one up the other day—a little blue book, which he showed me very secretly. I am at a loss to understand why Emberlin wishes to stamp out all trace of it. There is nothing to be ashamed of in the book; some of the verses, indeed, are, in their young ecstatic fashion, good. But they are certainly conceived in a style that is unlike that of his present poems. Perhaps it is that which makes him so implacable against them. What he writes now for very private manuscript circulation is curious stuff. I confess I prefer the earlier work; I do not like the stony, hard-edged quality of this sort of thing—the only one I can remember of his later productions. It is a sonnet on a porcelain figure of a woman, dug up at Cnossus:

> " Her eyes of bright unwinking glaze
> All imperturbable do not
> Even make pretences to regard
> The jutting absence of her stays

Where many a Syrian gallipot
Excites desire with spilth of nard.
The bistred rims above the fard
Of cheeks as red as bergamot
Attest that no shamefaced delays
Will clog fulfilment nor retard
Full payment of the Cyprian's praise
Down to the last remorseful jot.
Hail priestess of we know not what
Strange cult of Mycenean days! "

Regrettably, I cannot remember any of Emberlin's French poems. His peculiar muse expresses herself better, I think, in that language than in her native tongue.

Such is Emberlin; such, I should rather say, *was* he, for, as I propose to show, he is not now the man that he was when he whispered so confidentially to me, as I entered the room, that he had made a discovery about *Discoveries.*

I waited patiently till he had finished his little game of mystification and, when the moment seemed ripe, I asked him to explain himself. Emberlin was ready to open out.

"Well," he began, "these are the facts—a tedious introduction, I fear, but necessary. Years ago, when I was first reading Ben Jonson's *Discoveries,* that queer jotting of his, 'Eupompus gave splendour to Art by Numbers,' tickled my curiosity. You yourself must have been struck by the phrase, everybody must have noticed it; and everybody must have noticed too that no commentator has a word to say on the subject. That is the way of commentators—obvious points fulsomely explained and discussed, the hard passages, about which one might want to know something passed over in the silence of sheer ignorance. 'Eupompus gave splendour to Art by Numbers'—the absurd phrase stuck in my head. At one time it positively haunted me. I used to chant it in my bath, set to music as an anthem. It went like this, so far as I remember"—and he burst into song: "'Eupompus, Eu-u-pompus gave sple-e-e-endour...'" and so on, through all the repetitions, the dragged-out rises and falls of a parodied anthem.

"I sing you this," he said when he had finished, "just to show you what a hold that dreadful sentence took upon my mind. For eight years, off and on, its senselessness has besieged me. I have looked up Eupompus in all the obvious books of reference, of course. He is there all right—Alexandrian artist, eternized by some wretched little author in some even wretcheder little anecdote, which at the moment I entirely forget; it had nothing, at any rate, to do with the embellishment of art by numbers. Long ago I gave up the search as hopeless; Eupompus remained for me a shadowy figure of mystery, author of some nameless outrage, bestower of some forgotten benefit upon the art that he practiced. His history seemed wrapt in an impenetrable darkness. And then yesterday I discovered all about him and his art and his numbers. A chance discovery, than which few things have given me a greater pleasure.

"I happened upon it, as I say, yesterday when I was glancing through a volume of Zuylerius. Not, of course, the Zuylerius one knows," he added quickly, "otherwise one would have had the heart out of Eupompus' secret years ago."

"Of course," I repeated, "not the familiar Zuylerius."

"Exactly," said Emberlin, taking seriously my flippancy, "not the familiar John Zuylerius, Junior, but the elder Henricus Zuylerius, a much less—though perhaps undeservedly so—renowned figure than his son. But this is not the time to discuss their respective merits. At any rate, I discovered in a volume of critical dialogues by the elder Zuylerius, the reference, to which, without doubt, Jonson was referring in his note. (It was of course a mere jotting, never meant to be printed, but which Jonson's literary executors pitched into the book with all the rest of the available posthumous materials.) 'Eupompus gave splendour to Art by Numbers'—Zuylerius gives a very circumstantial account of the process. He must, I suppose, have found the sources for it in some writer now lost to us."

Emberlin paused a moment to muse. The loss of the work of any ancient writer gave him the keenest sorrow. I rather believe he had written a version of the unrecovered books of Petronius. Some day I hope I shall be permitted to see what conception Emberlin has of the *Satyricon* as a whole. He would, I am sure, do Petronius justice—almost too much, perhaps.

"What was the story of Eupompus?" I asked. "I am all curiosity to know."

Emberlin heaved a sigh and went on.

"Zuylerius' narrative," he said, "is very bald, but on the whole lucid; and I think it gives one the main points of the story. I will give it you in my own words; that is preferable to reading his Dutch Latin. Eupompus, then, was one of the most fashionable portrait-painters of Alexandria. His clientele was large, his business immensely profitable. For a half-length in oils the great courtesans would pay him a month's earnings. He would paint likenesses of the merchant princes in exchange for the costliest of their outlandish treasures. Coal-black potentates would come a thousand miles out of Ethiopia to have a miniature limned on some specially choice panel of ivory; and for payment there would be camel-loads of gold and spices. Fame, riches, and honor came to him while he was yet young; an unparalleled career seemed to lie before him. And then, quite suddenly, he gave it all up—refused to paint another portrait. The doors of his studio were closed. It was in vain that clients, however rich, however distinguished, demanded admission; the slaves had their order; Eupompus would see no one but his own intimates."

Emberlin made a pause in his narrative.

"What was Eupompus doing?" I asked.

"He was, of course," said Emberlin, "occupied in giving splendour to Art by Numbers. And this, as far as I can gather from Zuylerius, is how it all happened. He just suddenly fell in love with numbers—head over ears, amorous of pure counting. Number seemed to him to be the sole reality, the only thing about which the mind of man could be certain. To count was the one thing worth doing, because it was the one thing you could be sure of doing right. Thus, art, that it may have any value at all, must ally itself with reality—

must, that is, possess a numerical foundation. He carried the idea into practice by painting the first picture in his new style. It was a gigantic canvas, covering several hundred square feet—I have no doubt that Eupompus could have told you the exact area to an inch—and upon it was represented an illimitable ocean covered, as far as the eye could reach in every direction, with a multitude of black swans. There were thirty-three thousand of these black swans, each, even though it might be but a speck on the horizon, distinctly limned. In the middle of the ocean was an island, upon which stood a more or less human figure having three eyes, three arms and legs, three breasts and three navels. In the leaden sky three suns were dimly expiring. There was nothing more in the picture; Zuylerius describes it exactly. Eupompus spent nine months of hard work in painting it. The privileged few who were allowed to see it pronounced it, finished, a masterpiece. They gathered round Eupompus in a little school, calling themselves the Philarithmics. They would sit for hours in front of his great work, contemplating the swans and counting them; according to the Philarithmics, to count and to contemplate were the same thing.

"Eupompus' next picture, representing an orchard of identical trees set in quincunxes, was regarded with less favour by the connoisseurs. His studies of crowds were, however, more highly esteemed; in these were portrayed masses of people arranged in groups that exactly imitated the number and position of the stars making up various of the more famous constellations. And then there was his famous picture of the amphitheatre, which created a furore among the Philarithmics. Zuylerius again gives us a detailed description. Tier upon tier of seats are seen, all occupied by strange Cyclopean figures. Each tier accommodates more people than the tier below, and the number rises in a complicated but regular progression. All the figures seated in the amphitheatre possess but a single eye, enormous and luminous, planted in the middle of the forehead: and all these thousands of single eyes are fixed, in a terrible and menacing scrutiny, upon a dwarf-like creature cowering pitiably in the arena....He alone of the multitude possesses two eyes.

"I would give anything to see that picture," Emberlin added, after a pause. "The colouring, you know; Zuylerius gives no hint, but I feel somehow certain that the dominant tone must have been a fierce brick-red—a red granite amphitheatre filled with a red-robed assembly, sharply defined against an implacable blue sky."

" Their eyes would be green," I suggested.

Emberlin closed his eyes to visualize the scene and then nodded a slow and rather dubious assent.

"Up to this point," Emberlin resumed at length, Zuylerius' account is very clear. But his descriptions of the later philarithmic art become extremely obscure; I doubt whether he understood in the least what it was all about. I will give you such meaning as I manage to extract from his chaos. Eupompus seems to have grown tired of painting merely numbers of objects. He wanted now to represent Number itself. And then he conceived the plan of rendering visible the fundamental ideas of life through the medium of those purely numerical terms into which, according to him, they must ultimately resolve themselves. Zuylerius speaks vaguely of a picture of Eros, which seems to have consisted of a series of interlacing planes. Eupompus' fancy seems next to have been taken by various of the Socratic dialogues upon the nature of general ideas, and he made a series of illustrations for them in the same arithmogeometric style. Finally there is Zuylerius' wild description of the last picture that Eupompus ever painted. I can make very little of it. The subject of the work, at least, is clearly stated; it was a representation of Pure Number, or God and the Universe, or whatever you like to call that pleasingly inane conception of totality. It was a picture of the cosmos seen, I take it, through a rather Neoplatonic *camera obscura* very clear and in small. Zuylerius suggests a design of planes radiating out from a single point of light. I dare say something of the kind came in. Actually, I have no doubt, the work was a very adequate rendering in visible form of the conception of the one and the many, with all the intermediate stages of en-lightenment between matter and the *Fons Deitatis*. However, it's no use speculating what the picture may have been going to look like. Poor old Eupompus went mad before he had completely finished it and, after he had dispatched two of the admiring Philarithmics with a hammer, he flung himself out of the window and broke his neck. That was the end of him, and that was how he gave splendour, regrettably transient, to Art by Numbers."

Emberlin stopped. We brooded over our pipes in silence; poor old Eupompus!

That was four months ago, and today Emberlin is a confirmed and apparently irreclaimable Philarithmic, a quite whole-hearted Eupompian.

It was always Emberlin's way to take up the ideas that he finds in books and to put them into practice. He was once, for example, a working alchemist, and attained to considerable proficiency in the Great Art. He studied mnemonics under Bruno and Raymond Lully, and constructed for himself a model of the latter's syllogizing machine, in hopes of gaining that universal knowledge which the Enlightened Doctor guaranteed to its user. This time it is Eupompianism, and the thing has taken hold of him. I have held up to him all the hideous warnings that I can find in history. But it is no use.

There is the pitiable spectacle of Dr. Johnson under the tyranny of an Eupompian ritual, counting the posts and the paving-stones of Fleet Street. He himself knew best how nearly a madman he was.

And then I count as Eupompians all gamblers, all calculating boys, all interpreters of the prophecies of Daniel and the Apocalypse ; then too the Elberfeld horses, most complete of all Eupompians.

And here was Emberlin joining himself to this sect, degrading himself to the level of counting beasts and irrational children and men, more or less insane. Dr. Johnson was at least born with a strain of the Eupompian aberration in him; Emberlin is busily and consciously acquiring it. My expostulations, the expostulations of all his friends, are as yet unavailing. It is in vain that I tell Emberlin that counting is the easiest thing in the world to do, that when I am utterly exhausted, my brain, for lack of ability to perform any other work, just counts and reckons, like a machine, like an Elberfeld horse. It all falls on deaf ears; Emberlin merely smiles and shows me some new numerical joke that he has discovered. Emberlin can never enter a tiled bathroom now without counting how many courses of tiles there are from floor to ceiling. He regards it as an interesting fact that there are twenty-six rows of tiles in his bathroom and thirty-two in mine, while all the public lavatories in Holborn have the same number. He knows now how many paces it is from any one point in London to any other. I have given up going for walks with him. I am always made so distressingly conscious by his preoccupied look, that he is counting his steps.

His evenings, too, have become profoundly melancholy; the conversation, however well it may begin, always comes round to the same nauseating subject. We can never escape numbers; Eupompus haunts us. It is not as if we were mathematicians and could discuss problems of any interest or value. No, none of us are mathematicians, least of all Emberlin. Emberlin likes talking about such points as the numerical significance of the Trinity, the immense importance of its being three in one, not forgetting the even greater importance of its being one in three. He likes giving us statistics about the speed of light or the rate of growth in fingernails. He loves to speculate on the nature of odd and even numbers. And he seems to be unconscious how much he has changed for the worse. He is happy in an exclusively absorbing interest. It is as though some mental leprosy had fallen upon his intelligence.

In another year or so, I tell Emberlin, he may almost be able to compete with the calculating horses on their own ground. He will have lost all traces of his reason, but he will be able to extract cube roots in his head. It occurs to me that the reason why Eupompus killed himself was not that he was mad; on the contrary, it was because he was, temporarily, sane. He had been mad for years, and then suddenly the idiot's self-complacency was lit up by a flash of sanity. By its momentary light he saw into what gulfs of imbecility he had plunged. He saw and understood, and the full horror, the lamentable absurdity of the situation made him desperate. He vindicated Eupompus against Eupompianism, humanity against the Philarithmics. It gives me the greatest pleasure to think that he disposed of two of that hideous crew before he died himself.

Reprinted from *Limbo* (New York: George H. Doran Company, 1920).

Lojze Kovačič (Slovenia)

Born in 1928 in Basel, Switzerland, Lojze Ko-
vačič, born of Slovenian-German parents, arrived
in Slovenia before the Second World War at the
age of ten. He learned Slovenian and began writ-
ing social realist stories, but shifted quickly to a
more subjective and modernist style of writing.
He is the winner of numerous awards, and is
now considered the doyen of Slovenian prose.
Among his major works are Pet fragmentov
(Five Fragments) of 1981 and the two-volume
novel Prišleki *(Newcomers), written from 1984*
to 1985. Until his retirement, he worked as a
mentor in puppet theater workshops.

A Story of the Dead Ljudmila

She was a wicked mother who always prevented her daughter Ljudmila from going out.
She even denied her a mirror in the house.
Thus the daughter admired her beauty in the
stream behind the house or in the Krka,
where cattle were watered. On the other side
of the Krka lived Jurij. He had no faith in God
nor a vocation and would say he needed
none. By night he would follow the path of
the moon, from beginning to end, and spin
his hat on a beanpole. He was a lay-about,
worse than gypsies. Those would at least,
now and then, drag rocks from the quarry. He
chose neither evil nor holy for to him both
were intangible, but he also knew not what
good meant. When people said, "Jur, you are
like a beast," he just nodded and sunk his
head on his chest like a raven in want of rest.
At the wicked mother's place his name was
not to be mentioned and when the mother
beat Ljudmila with an oxwhip because the
girl thought of Jurij, she, too, did it without a

word. One night, having greased the hinges, Ljudmila sneaked out and ran across the dam at the watering-place to the other side of the Krka. Amid the willows Jurij waited. He spun his hat on the beanpole and flung it on Ljudmila's head. Then, in the shadow of the big hat it happened what was bound to happen. On Ljudmila's return the door did not creak. To her mother, though, it sufficed to find, on the morrow, a leaf in her daughter's bed, laying like a man's hand in the midst of the sheet. The wicked mother did not weep. Deftly she made a fire under a big copper cauldron and asked the Virgin Mary for her permission. As Ljudmila came by and looked into the cauldron to get a glimpse of her face on the surface, she saw the black leaf at the bottom. And at that moment her mother pushed her into the scalding water, where her beauty and all trace of life were lost.

Her grave was still new when at night Jur stole in. He dug out Ljudmila's corpse, laid her into the grass, spread her arms and legs and took her, but not before he had cast a spell, whereupon the crosses and tombstones in the graveyard of Prečna shook and crashed into each other with infernal noise. After that Ljudmila could speak and hear again and could, like living souls, perform all the necessary tasks of her seeming life, not a shade different from a real one. She shivered with cold and Jur covered her with his big hat. Together they followed the path of the moon and finally stopped in the mountains, at a remote place, where Ljudmila could hide her death. Soon, Jur found a job and began to live like others. At first Ljudmila kept to the house for fear the community might guess she was dead, but after a while she herself forgot her true condition.

On Thursdays she would wash, on Fridays fast and iron linen, and her speech became like the speech of others. The village women came and brought her their pastry. In return, she offered them her home-made jam. With Jur she lived on The Slope; at noon their house smelt of bread and on the pasture downhill their cow bellowed. For Easter Ljudmila went to the village fair, bought some pigfat, a hanky with a woven lily and woolen socks for her beloved. At the fair there was an accordionist, who roamed about the country, playing merry tunes. At this place of mirth, Jur coming from work met Ljudmila at a market-stall. They danced to the music of the accordion and to the sound of the accordion they went home. When they were gone the music ceased and the fair grew silent. But through the accordionist all was disclosed. He made a long detour to reach the wicked mother's house and recount that at the fair he had seen Ljudmila in Jur's embrace, neither of them afraid of the holy Easter bells. The wicked mother gave him bread and meat and threw him out without a word. At dusk she went to Ignatius, the priest. No sooner did she enter the vicarage than the whole parish darkened. Ignatius was in a gay mood and drunk but his laughter turned into squeals under the wicked mother's eve, as he learned how her daughter had fooled death. The wicked mother urged him to call Ljudmila's place to see the truth for himself and bring her back to her home in the churchyard. The vicar, however, was rather lazy and it took guile on the part of the mother him realize that she was serious.

So, on the following day he took his carriage loaded with a bread-chest, in truth coffin in disguise, and drove to his destination. As he appeared at the foot of the hill, Ljudmila knew she could hide her death no more. The priest sat down at the kitchen table and the young woman brought him some home-brewed brandy. Now he saw she was with child. He burst into laughter, as he oft did— but not in spite, for the latter he confined only to his sleep. He laughed because the human muddle reminded him anew that the whole world was turned upside down once and for all. But then, he was well, feasting on bread and brandy, the place was cosy and he weary, so instead of calling Ljudmila the Devil's bride, he said, "Dear girl, what has smitten you to have got yourself into this state?" Instead of railing at Ljudmila, "You flesh, rotten from death," he just smiled, "You have plumped out prettily." Still, at the height of his weary delirium, a moment of reluctant sobriety came and he mumbled, "Your mother would rather have you dead that tied to forbidden love." To which Ljudmila replied, "But my mother killed me." Ignatius, the priest, turning a deaf ear to any doubt, only smiled remorsefully, handing her his empty glass, "Yes, one more, gladly." In gloomy resignation, which is alike for the living and the dead, Ljudmila poured him another brandy. Without saying much, she was yielding slowly to death. From a drawer she took her funeral shirt, neatly washed and ironed, smelling of lavender. She put it on and took her rosary. She made her face white with some powder she had purchased at the fair, but could have done without for her face grew paler and paler each minute. Then she lay down in the large bread-chest brought by Ignatius, the priest, on his carriage, and folded her arms. The vicar nailed up the chest, and she saw how his hands were shaking and was sorry for him. The priest, too, pitied himself, though the trembling did not come from emotion but the exhaustion of old age.

The long carriage ride over the stony winding roads lolled Ljudmila, shut in the bread-chest; she began a labor. The wicked mother, all the same, bade that more nails be driven into the lid. And when Ljudmila was lowered into a deep, fort-like grave and Ignatius, the priest, wept with fatigue, a joyous cry of the new-born baby rose out of the coffin.

Reprinted from *The Imagination of Terra Incognita: Slovenian Writing 1945-1995* (Fredonia, New York; White Pine Press, 1997), story translated by Miriam Drev. Reprinted by permission of White Pine Press.

1001 Great Stories

Niccolò Tucci (b.Italy/USA)

Born in Italy in 1908, Niccolò Tucci began by writing his fiction in Italian, but after emigrating to the United States in the 1930s, started writing in English, publishing in numerous periodicals of the day, including Partisan Review, Harper's, The Atlantic, *and* The New Yorker.

The Rain Came Last and Other Stories, *from which the story "Hey!" is reprinted, was the first collection of Tucci's English-language stories to be published. Among his several books are, in Italian,* Il Segreto, *winner of the Viareggio Prize in 1956,* Gli Antlantici, *winner of the Bagutta Prize in 1968, and* Confessioni Involontarie *(1975). His English-language works include* Before My Time *(1962),* Unfinished Funeral *(1964), and* The Sun and the Moon *(1977).*

Hey!

The place was called Siberia: fifteen miles
from Florence, smaller than the Russian
Siberia and less cold, but a bad place all the
same. Green and hot in the summer, almost
constantly flooded in winter by one, two or
all of the six torrents crossing the plain of Pis-
toia between high embankments. In mild
winters the floods lasted only a few weeks,
then for another few weeks the mud was so
thick that our light two-wheeled buggy became as heavy as a cart loaded with stones. If
the winter was dry, the furrows of the last
carriage on the road remained imprinted like
canyons in a relief-map, and whoever ven-
tured in his carriage on that road ran the risk
of breaking axle and springs and of being
thrown off his seat. And once you started on
the road there was no way back. Almost all
roads in the plain ran between two deep irri-
gation canals, and if you met another carriage
it was either for you or for him to pass with
one wheel down the slope, very often tipping

over. Even from far away you could hear those yells: "Haaaay-hooo.... Stop there.... Eee-up, eeeeee-upp!" followed by curses in the best Tuscan tradition.

I remember Tesi, who lived in Siberia, because he had built our garden and worked as a handyman for us until he became too weak from tuberculosis and knew it was time for him to go home and die. Father tried to get him to go to the hospital, but he refused. When he understood that he was going to be helped against his will, he said we had better stop interfering, because if he saw an ambulance on the road to his house, he would shoot. That is why, although there was no hope for him, Father decided to go and see him during the winter, every three or four days. He lived in a house that looked like an ancient Roman ruin, although it was only some forty years old. Haystack, plough, chicken-coop, a long, narrow cornfield in front of the house and the greyish wall of Mangoni's house beyond the vineyard: that was his view. Mangoni had a bigger house and a bigger family. He didn't own his strip of land like Tesi; it belonged to the rich bachelor Baldi, but like Tesi and everybody in every house along those dirt roads, he was visited by tuberculosis. Only his folk died more slowly, without all sorts of complications such as bronchitis or pneumonia.

I usually went with Father to see Tesi. I liked the adventure of wading, the noise of water on the wheels, the trees reflected in the water, and the solitude. While my father visited his patient, I covered up the horse with a red blanket, gave it a little hay, and read a book or studied my Latin or my botany. When it rained I sat in the kitchen beside the fire. Like all peasant kitchens, it had a smoky pot of water hanging on a black chain in the fireplace, and the rest of the room was only a little lighter than the pot and the chain. I remember a yellow leaflet nailed to the wall, dotted by millions of fly excrements. It read: "WHAT GOD THINKS OF WOMAN," and it said that God hated immodesty, adultery, bad language and laxity in religious practices. There were also a few illustrated post cards with views of towns under deep blue skies, almost completely blackened by the flies, too. In one corner there was an oil lamp in front of a post card of a Madonna, framed with a piece of paper lace.

I still don't know why the sound of Tesi's coughing upstairs had the quality of rotting wood. Perhaps because I associated it with the rotting beams that by some sort of miracle held up the ceiling, or perhaps because in that small house all voices became encased, absorbed by the holes in the wood, so that only the ghost of a voice is allowed to reach your ear.

My conversations with Tesi's wife were very difficult, because, for fear of inhaling dirty microbes, I kept my lips tightly closed, I had gone near many a wealthy t.b. patient without being afraid of anything, so it was really the dirty microbes that I minded. But even if I had been willing to talk, she never said a word, except—"O my God," or "O, what a world..." or simply, "Ooooh." And looking at the house or listening to her husband cough, there was indeed little I could say that wouldn't have sounded silly. Her name, strangely enough, was Gorilla. She came from one of the many Gori families and there were several girls named Gorilla Gori. I recall sitting in Gorilla's company for hours, watching the rain on the three deformed stones of the steps to the house door, or the undulant floor of the kitchen itself, with here and there a brick missing and all the other bricks caved in or broken into such small pieces that they looked like the wrinkles on her face. I never saw much of her face: a large brown kerchief, with the two ends going out right and left from under her chin, left just an oval opening, a sort of window, for her face. In there she was: a ravaged forehead with furrows in all directions, two dark eyes with much white around them, and a long nose.

They had two children: Isaia and Manno, strange creatures who frightened me. Isaia was nine or ten, perhaps even twelve, they didn't know; and Manno was six. But there was hardly any difference between them in size: probably all they had to exhibit in the line of growth, all their reserves of cells or whatever it is that makes people strong, didn't reach beyond the age of six. After six they began to shrink as science teaches us normal people do at thirty-five. They both had large, shiny foreheads; the skin was tight as parchment on a drum. Their voices were hardly audible, and rattled drily, like wood, when they spoke. But their laughter was ghastly, as if it were beyond their voices: it took place in the region of sighs and coughs. Father said that was the "voce afona," the toneless voice of t.b. patients, and whenever I heard them play I hoped they wouldn't come near me, for I felt like crying out of sheer compassion. They always looked at my sad face with amused curiosity, however, then fled from me to "laugh" among themselves.

I remember that Father once told Tesi that his children should not sleep in the same bed with him, and he asked whether it would be better for them to sleep outside the window. All the peasants kept their children with them when they were ill. In Tesi's house there was only one room upstairs with a big bed in it. On that bed a child was conceived, born or "sbucciato," as they say in Tuscany, that is, peeled: shown the facts of life in a few visual lessons, then shown how one dies of the family disease, and left to do it when the time was ripe for the performance. After the big storm broke the tree outside the house and it fell on the roof, breaking the tiles, they made up a bed of clothes and sacks of corn in a corner for the children, and when it rained Tesi held an umbrella over himself in bed. The big green umbrella under which Tesi had come to our house hundreds of times in the past was very convenient: it took the few drops that leaked through the roof and splashed them in the direction of the stairway. Thus the bed remained dry.

In the spring Gorilla became ill too, and the children had to be sent to the Mangoni's where they slept in the stable. In the daytime they played in the fields as usual. They didn't even have to feed their donkey, because Mangoni had taken it into his stable. But once a day they greeted their parents, "Hey!" Just opening the door and shouting "Hey!" inside the kitchen. The two patients didn't have to reply, because every attempt to shout brought forth a violent access of coughing which usually ended in that lacerating "Gooo goo aaaht," preceding blood-spitting, or as the doctors call it, emottisis. The Billi woman from San Michele stayed with them practically all day now. She fed them and helped them defecate. The rest of the time she sat in the kitchen, knitting away at her straw hats which in those days still sold quite well in America, and every now and then she threw a strange glance at the poverty around her, as if to make sure that no one had stolen it.

We had a few beautiful days in February, so beautiful that everybody said, "This is real spring now" (and it was); and then rain and rain for two months without one single day of respite. And Siberia was awful then. But Father went there anyway, because Tesi enjoyed talking to him. Father was funny: he hated to see patients; he had no faith in medicine anyway, but he liked Tesi because with him it was all a relationship beyond disease; if anything medical was mentioned it was only to get the conversation started or to fill a gap in it. One day I heard Tesi inquire about my brothers, my sister and myself; I heard him pronounce each name distinctly, very slowly, and my father give him the description of our "exceptional qualities" he usually reserved for guests of distinction. It was strange to hear him talk that way in the stone hut, in the midst of such desolate flooded country. It brought the light atmosphere of a drawing-room there; to me it was like a dream. Tesi tried to say something like, "I am so glad," but when he came to the word "so," he stumbled into the most desperate series of choking coughs. Gorilla never said a word, letting the men talk, but I was sure that she was listening from her side of the bed.

On May second (birthday of Leonardo da Vinci, born in the house down there on the slope of that grey hill) the rain stopped and the clouds went away. Corn, wheat, vines, and just simple grass on the edge of the fields were so green against the sunshine that it filled me with the usual despair: never could such green be told by anyone. The two patients were dying; it was hard to tell who would die first; Gorilla had made good progress in two months and was by now nearly as ill as Tesi. Father's visits lasted much longer now, because Tesi kept asking him about medicine, geography, history, botany; at home I had collected a few illustrated magazines and books for Father to show him and burn afterwards. Father was giving him an education. He enjoyed it. Once I saw him from the haystack: he was holding a white sheet of paper over Tesi's bed, describing the functioning of the heart. He had made the same drawing in my notebook only a few days before. I didn't mind those long visits; I sat in the carriage with my book open on my knees but couldn't read. I kept looking at the leaves against the sunshine. I listened to the birds, to distant church bells, I inhaled the new earth, the smell of horses, cows, flowers, and was drunk with poetry. The only thing that disturbed me was when the children came, because they seemed to like the game of yelling "Hey!" into the house. Their toneless call into that dark receptacle of death destroyed everything around me; even the sun itself seemed affected by it.

One day Father appeared at the window in his white attire and asked me to take the horse away from under the fig tree and to stand in front of the horse, holding the reins. I wondered why, but obeyed. After a few seconds I heard a shot, then another one, and I saw a branch of the fig tree fall to the ground. The barrel of a gun was still resting on the window-sill. My father explained later that for a few days Tesi had been longing to shoot. He was a good huntsman, but the season was far off. He didn't care; he just wanted to bring about a change in the view: a large fig leaf had stood right in the middle of his field of vision; he had looked at it for hours and hours and now he wanted to shoot it. It made him feel as if he had gone out and got something done. But after a second experiment Father forbade him to shoot again and taught him more about the world instead.

I had become so familiar with the idea of those two patients that now I was anxious to see whether there was an end to human resistance; it was pure scientific curiosity. On a Wednesday towards the end of May, not a

clear day, not a clean sky, but just hot and unpleasant, Father said: "This is the day. We
won't find them alive. I think they will die at
almost the same moment. But we shall go
there anyway, because from there we must go
to Mangoni's. One of his daughters had a
strong emottisis last night."

I would have wanted to go upstairs with
my father, but I didn't dare ask him. Would
they die coughing, or would they yell, or just
whistle like the wind under a door? Had I
been going to keep a date with a girl, I could
hardly have been more impatient or more
afraid of being discovered by my father. I
drove the carriage beyond the fig tree so I
could look into the room. I stepped on the
seat, but couldn't see much; a white form, the
bed, but nothing to indicate that it wasn't
empty. Yes, the whistle, not so much like the
wind under a door as like crickets in the first
evening of summer. Such a sweet sound usually awoke in me nostalgic dreams or fiery de-
sires: how horrible to hear it from the lips of
a dying man. Why didn't I hear his wife, too?
Was she dead? I saw my father pass in front

of the window and bend over the bed. I blushed and jumped off the seat, but he hadn't seen me. Then I saw the Billi woman standing by the horse.

I had to explain, "I thought my father was calling me and I wondered why."

"No, he wasn't," she said and sighed, knitting away as usual at her straw braids.

The Mangoni woman came across the fields, followed by three girls. They were all knitting and all curious.

"Your father is coming to my place after this," she said.

And I said, "Yes, we are."

"The priest is due any minute," said the Billi woman. In fact, the bells of San Michele were just beginning to touch off the monotonous hammering of the occasion.

"She," said the Mangoni woman, "was dead half an hour ago."

"Oh," said the Billi woman. "So it's only he who still has to finish his suffering. Well, rich or poor..." and she went nearer the house to hear better.

Isaia and Manno appeared from the street,

barefoot as usual, dirty, covered with dust as if they had been in a baker-shop. They were walking, each with a hand on the other's shoulder, and seemed to be having a good time.

"Shhhhh!" said the two women, and made a sign for them to go away. But they came up to the horse and began giggling stupidly. Then Isaia said something to his brother who ran like the devil to the house, jumped lightly up the three steps, pushed the door open and shouted, "Hey, hey, hey...!" until the woman ran after him, grabbed him by his frail arm and threw him back to the middle of the yard, saying, "Shame! They are dying in there."

But Isaia laughed. In that province of laughter foreign to his voice, he emitted painful whistles from his open mouth. He sounded like his father and went on laughing that way, beating his knees with his hands, then pointing to his brother with a long, dark, bony finger, and groaning: "I fooled him! I fooled him!"

Reprinted from *The Rain Came Last and Other Stories*
(New York: New Directions, 1990). ©1945, 1947, 1948,
1949, 1950, 1957, 1958, 1950, 1990 by Niccolò Tucci.
Reprinted by permission of New Directions Publishing
Corporation.

GREEN INTEGER
Pataphysics and Pedantry

Douglas Messerli, Publisher

Essays, Manifestos, Statements, Speeches, Maxims,
Epistles, Diaristic Notes, Narratives, Natural Histories,
Poems, Plays, Performances, Ramblings, Revelations
and all such ephemera as may appear necessary
to bring society into a slight tremolo of confusion
and fright at least.

*

Individuals may order Green Integer titles through PayPal
(www.Paypal.com). Please pay the price listed below plus $2.00
for postage to Green Integer through the PayPal system.
You can also visit our site at www.greeninteger.com
If you have questions please feel free to e-mail
the publisher at info@greeninteger.com
Bookstores and libraries should order through our distributors:
USA and Canada: Consortium Book Sales and Distribution
1045 Westgate Drive, Suite 90, Saint Paul, Minnesota 55114-1065
United Kingdom and Europe: Turnaround Publisher Services
Unit 3, Olympia Trading Estate, Coburg Road, Wood Green,
London N22 6TZ UK

*

OTHER TITLES [LISTED BY AUTHOR]

Amelia Rosselli *War Variations* [1-931243-55-7] $14.95
Tiziano Rossi *People on the Run* [1-931243-37-9] $12.95
Sappho *Poems* [1-892295-13-X] $10.95

Mark Wallace *Temporary Worker Rides a Subway*
    [1-931243-60-3] $10.95
Barrett Watten *Frame (1971-1990)* [Sun & Moon Press:
    1-55713-239-9] $13.95
        Progress / Under Erasure [1-931243-68-9] $12.95
Mac Wellman *Crowtet 1: A Murder of Crows and
        The Hyacinth Macaw* [1-892295-52-0] $11.95
        Crowtet 2: Second-Hand Smoke and The Lesser Magoo
        [1-931243-71-9] $12.95
        The Land Beyond the Forest: Dracula and Swoop
        [Sun & Moon Press: 1-55713-228-3] $12.95
Oscar Wilde *The Critic As Artist* [1-55713-328-x] $9.95
William Carlos Williams *The Great American Novel*
        [1-931243-52-2] $10.95
Yang Lian *Yi* [1-892295-68-7] $14.95
Yi Ch'ŏngjun *Your Paradise* [1-931243-69-7] $13.95
Visar Zhiti *The Condemned Apple: Selected Poetry*
    [1-931243-72-7] $10.95

† Author winner of the Nobel Prize for Literature
± Author winner of the America Award for Literature
• Book translation winner of the PEN American Center Translation
  Award [PEN-West]
* Book translation winner of the PEN/Book-of-the-Month Club
  Translation Prize
+ Book translation winner of the PEN Award for Poetry
  in Translation

The America Awards

FOR A LIFETIME CONTRIBUTION TO INTERNATIONAL WRITING
Awarded by the Contemporary Arts Educational Project, Inc.
in loving memory of Anna Fahrni

The 2006 Award winner is:

JULIEN GRACQ (LOUIS POIRIER)

[FRANCE] 1910

Previous winners:

1994 AIMÉ CESAIRE [Martinique] 1913
1995 HAROLD PINTER [England] 1930
1996 JOSÉ DONOSO [Chile] 1924-1996 (awarded prior to his death)
1997 FRIEDERIKE MAYRÖCKER [Austria] 1924
1998 RAFAEL ALBERTI [Spain] 1902-1998 (awarded prior to his death)
1999 JACQUES ROUBAUD [France] 1932
2000 EUDORA WELTY [USA] 1909-2001
2001 INGER CHRISTENSEN [Denmark] 1935
2002 PETER HANDKE [Austria] 1942
2003 ADONIS [Syria/Lebanon] 1930
2004 JOSÉ SARAMAGO [Portugal] 1922
2005 ANDREA ZANZOTTO [Italy] 1921

The rotating panel for The America Awards currently consists of Douglas
Messerli [chairman], Will Alexander, Luigi Ballerini, Peter Constantine,
Peter Glassgold, Deborah Meadows, Martin Nakell, John O'Brien, Mar-
jorie Perloff, Joe Ross, Jerome Rothenberg, Paul Vangelisti, and Mac
Wellman.